DATE DUE

MAY 2 2 2008		Arrival Date	

DEMCO 38-296

UNCERTAIN PILGRIMS

UNCERTAIN PILGRIMS

A NOVEL

LENORE CARROLL

University of New Mexico Press | Albuquerque

PRINTED IN THE UNITED STATES OF AMERICA
10 09 08 07 06   1 2 3 4 5

LIBRARY OF CONGRESS CATALOGING-IN-PUBLICATION DATA
Carroll, Lenore, 1939–
    Uncertain pilgrims / Lenore Carroll.
        p. cm.
    ISBN-13: 978-0-8263-3566-1 (ALK. PAPER)
    ISBN-10: 0-8263-3566-7 (ALK. PAPER)
    1. Santa Fe National Historic Trail—Fiction. I. Title.

    PS3553.A7648U53 2006
    813'.54—dc22

                        2005031406

ℰℴ

Chapter two previously appeared as "Sojourn in
    Kansas" in Robert Randisi, ed., *White Hat*
    (Berkeley Books, 2002).

Chapter six previously appeared as "Traveling
    Princess" in Loren Estleman, ed., *American
    West: Twenty New Stories* (New York:
    Forge, 2001).

Chapter eleven previously appeared as "Letter
    Home" in Lee Shultz, ed., *RE:AL*, Stephen F.
    Austin State University (spring 1991).

ℰℴ

Book and cover design and type composition, Kathleen Sparkes.

This book is typeset using Trump Mediaeval 10.5/15; 25P6.

Display type is the Minion family.

To Max Evans,
for encouraging me.
You raised the bar
for the rest of us.

Contents

PROLOGUE

~

I always felt better once I was past Topeka, off the official Kansas Turnpike. No more toll booths. I escaped the pull of home and now it would be easy to keep going. I felt okay as long as I was moving, the car humming, roads rolling by.

I was escaping and as long as my car ran, as long as I put in gas and oil and replaced tires, I could get away from my life. I could escape the hard facts and the cold memories. No job, no man, no child, no father. Who wouldn't want to run away?

Between classical selections, Kansas Public Radio reminded me it was Midsummer Day. Would sturdy Midwestern witches dance in the woods tonight? The year balanced on a moment of longest light, each day to come shorter than the last. Was this an auspicious time to travel? The cloud of gloom over my head and the damp, drizzly November in my soul competed with the midsummer glare on the wheat fields. I'd travel through the geographic center of the country squinting at the sun in my eyes.

I'd left Kansas City, the home of regional offices, 90 percent humidity, 800 feet elevation, mixed woods and grasslands, average everything, to be viewed with irony and nostalgia. I was headed for

Santa Fe, New Age Vatican, 20 percent humidity, 7,200 feet elevation, high plains desert and mountains, to be viewed with awe and interest. I was on my way to Elsewhere. I followed the Santa Fe Trail, with no goal and no reason to return. Kansas City—actually Independence and Westport—were historic jumping-off places for the trails. I had jumped off into the unknown, my trek down the trail in an old but reliable Honda, not a Conestoga. I packed a tent and some camping gear, clothes, and credit cards. I'd stop at the historic army forts on the way to Santa Fe, to worship at the minor shrines, then at Santa Fe itself, history cathedral. Then Somewhere Else.

I had outlived the Hour of Lead, as Emily described it, when Nerves sit ceremonious like Tombs. I drove with stiff heart, mechanical feet. Kevin had left without waiting to meet his daughter, Antonia, the wonder baby who had conquered my parents' hearts. Then she died in her crib. It was too much for my father and he joined her. Then my mother wrapped herself in her other grandchildren. I managed to get myself fired from Sprint, the best place to work in Kansas City. I'd been so out of it with my personal tragedies, I hadn't done much but show up. My brain was stuck on Feeling; no Thinking took place. Coping was the best I could do. What would this look like on my resume? Fuck resume. What did this look like in my life?

I should have told them what was wrong—then I'd be officially nuts—but instead I did too good a job of denial and didn't Get Professional Help in time. Eventually, I tired of being bright and phony; the pretending was too hard. My shrink said I had issues with self-esteem I needed to deal with. I'd dealt, but the hand was aces and eights.

Days of lead, lead sneakers, lead jacket, lead stiff heart. Everything in my life gray and dead for so long, I didn't know what else there was. When they put you in the hospital to regulate your meds, it's clinical. Now I hoped I could outrun melancholy.

Maybe the western sun would burn through the lead. Maybe the wind would wear it away, the way it wore away rock with grains of sand. I could drive and it felt like progress even though I wasn't sure where the ending was.

Everybody has heartbreaks, my aunt Catherine said. Pull yourself together and get on with your life. I was tired of trying to hold myself together. I'd drive 'til I was exhausted, 'til I maxed out my cards, then I'd let go and see if I came apart. I'd drive until food had taste again. Until I heard each note of a bird song. Until my mouth watered when I smelled dinner. Until I could bear a man's hand on my body, and my body's response. If I drove long enough, the lead would melt. In the meantime I could pass for normal, conduct a conversation, smile and nod. And retreat if it got hard.

My mother thought I was running away from my emotions. She didn't know those long empty hours of driving just gave them space. I could sort through what had happened. I had all the time in the world. I knew what I was running from; maybe I could work out how to go on.

I wanted a man in my life, someone who would give me a reason to be alive, another person I could share with. I wanted children to absorb the love I wanted to give. I didn't think I would find either on this trip, but I'd have time to work out how to get what I needed.

I would follow the Santa Fe Trail across July Kansas, baking hot and tawny with dust. I would pretend I was some doughty pioneer or some proper army officer's wife, pinch-faced and solemn in daguerreotype. I would indulge my history addiction, dawdle at the historical sites, lose myself in time and place. The stories have a strong hold on me for reasons I can't explain; sometimes they are more real than my life. They can't change; they can't surprise me; they can't betray me. I can take refuge in them. Something about the stories grabs me and I read through to the end.

It's a harmless hobby. I could have collected china salt and pepper shakers or become an Internet junkie, but I wanted out of my head and into fresh air. I set my cruise control for seventy and aimed for northern New Mexico, where Penitentes atoned for the big death from Los Alamos mesa.

My first stop had been at Fort Leavenworth for the Transportation Museum. I shouldn't have been surprised to run into another history buff.

CHAPTER ONE
FORT LEAVENWORTH

❧

2000

I hesitated at the door into the Transportation Museum displays, a space as big as an airplane hangar.

Wanting to know about army wives probably said something about me, but I hadn't a clue what it might be. What did I hope to find in their stories?

When I walked into the museum I breathed concrete, old wood, motor oil, unused space.

The first time I stumbled on a memoir by one of the army wives—Mrs. Boyd or Mrs. Lane—I imagined myself there: harsh southwestern wind blowing my long skirts, the endless sky stretching blue forever. My great-grandfather had come over from Sicily in steerage to Galveston, then north on the Kansas City, Galveston and Mexico City Railroad. Where did I get this sense of having been in the Southwest?

Now I stood in front of an 1870s Spring Wagon, just like the one that had taken Mrs. Boyd and her Chinese servant through Apache country.

I studied the enlarged photo on display: a proper nineteenth-century army family. Two dozen closely spaced buttons held the wife's stiffly corseted bodice closed. Stiff curls lay flat to her forehead. She looked stern, one hand resting on the baby. The baby looked blurred, in the wicker carriage, covered with a fringed shawl, the mustachioed father stiff and correct in his kepi and tunic with shoulder boards. The long exposure time of those old photographs meant the subjects had to hold still. They were probably funny people who laughed and joked, but in their photos they are solemn.

The Spring Wagon didn't look big enough. The leather driver's seat faced ahead; the other seats faced each other. No aisle, but entry through a door on the side. It was shiny with paint and sported red fringe and the canvas sides were rolled up. Mrs. Boyd could brace the champagne basket, which held the baby, on the floor between the seats. I wondered how rough the ride was over trail ruts. The vehicle looked lightweight, like a city vehicle.

The sign on the display was a perfect introduction to my journey in search of women's stories:

"The Girl I Left Behind Me"
—A traditional air played as the troops left the post.
    The frontier army wife came from the middle class of the settled East and brought her civilizing influence to bear on isolated posts and the men stationed there. The sentiment of the Frontier Army wife was described by Frances Roe when she said, "Yes we are sometimes called 'camp followers' but we do not mind . . . it probably originated with some envious bachelor officer. We know all about the comfort and cheer that goes with us, and then we have not been left behind."

My life couldn't have been more different—growing up in a large Sicilian family that once lived in the North End of Kansas City. We still gathered at Grandma Zita's on holidays, when everybody told everybody else what was on his mind. It was great, unless you'd done something they didn't like. Since my dad died, they'd left me alone. Although my circumstances were different, I knew how those nineteenth-century women felt. Being separated from their families. Starting a new life. Having children. I probably had been an army wife in some previous incarnation.

I wandered through this museum to the back, where old wagons and carriages were ranked in an indoor parking lot. My preoccupation with movement and traveling latched onto those nineteenth-century vehicles. I was happily lost until men's voices disturbed me.

"See here," said a blustery old man, "George Armstrong himself sat on that seat."

A man who looked like a younger, more compact version of the older man nodded.

"Why, him and that purty little wife rode on these very streets," the old man enthused.

I stiffened. That wasn't quite right. "He ordered it, but he didn't pay for it," I spoke up. "Sheridan called him back before his year's punishment for the court martial was over."

"It says here," insisted the old man, "that it was Custer's special order."

"That doesn't mean he ever rode in it." *Why did I have to open my mouth?* "Besides, why should the carriage maker let him have it without paying?"

The younger man smiled as he listened.

"You ever bought anything on time, Sis?" the old man countered.

I sheepishly had to agree that I had, thinking of the payments on my CRX outside.

"I'm Dale Jackson from Independence and this here's my son, Tom."

I shook hands and introduced myself. "Carla Brancato."

"I haven't been up here," Dale recalled, "since they had a show in eighty-eight or eighty-seven of photographs this woman took of the Santa Fe Trail, the ones they put in the book."

"You're interested in the trail?" I asked.

"You bet," said Dale.

The three of us strolled around the exhibits, exchanging views on the vehicles. Dale and I discussed the information on the signs and the items on display. Son Tom seemed interested enough, but it was obvious the historical minutiae weren't his thing.

After almost an hour, we circled back to the Spring Wagon display. I told Dale how much I enjoyed the army wives' memoirs and confided, "I'd give anything to get inside that wagon, just to feel what it was like."

Dale looked around, saw no one, and unhooked the rope. I shook my head.

"Go ahead, Sis. Nobody'll know."

I was too embarrassed to speak and sort of waved my hands for him to quit.

"I'll go see about it," said Dale, and he started for the front door.

"Please, I don't think they let you—" I looked helplessly at his son.

He just shrugged.

One of the women from the gift shop led Dale to an office near the front door and they disappeared.

"That's very nice of your father," I said. But I resented having to wait to see what would happen.

"Dad can be overbearing at times. You have to be firm or he'll run right over you."

"You don't seem to mind."

"I'm used to him. I go along with his history thing. What do you see in it?"

"It's hard to put into words. I love the stories from the past and when I see something—a room, a wagon, a photograph—it sends me back in time."

Dale reappeared with a man in summer clothes, who smiled.

"I have to stay here," the curator said, "but go ahead." And he opened the rope. I kicked off my shoes and stepped into the wagon. The springs gave under my weight and the wagon bounced a little. My heart speeded up. I caressed the black painted wood, tugged the door open, and sat inside. I heard the harness jingle and the leather creak. I felt the jerk and jostle as the steel-rimmed wheels rolled over the Kansas prairie. I smelled dust and horses and human sweat. My three petticoats cushioned me a little, but I had to hold onto the side to keep my balance. Outriders called and the captain shouted orders to the troopers. The wind held rain and there would be a thunderstorm before morning. I reached for my carryall.

"How's it feel, Sis?" Dale asked.

"Like home," I said without thinking.

I backed down the steps and thanked the curator profusely. I told Dale, "You embarrassed me to death, but I'm glad you did. How did you know I wanted to do that?"

"Why wouldn't you?" he answered.

Tom smiled and shook his head. "He's done this all my life. It was terrible when I was a teenager."

"Teenagers are easily embarrassed." I remembered.

"We were planning to grab an early lunch at that Pizza Hut just outside the gates, Sis. Why don't you come along?"

"Sure, thanks." They looked harmless enough and it was rare that I found other people interested in the same history I was. I was the only woman under forty in the local Posse of the Westerners. I had spent some energy getting ready for this trip; now, it felt okay just to let it happen.

When I got back from the ladies' room, I heard the volunteer behind the counter in the museum shop saying, "We lived in Greece and then Germany and my kids had lived out of the States more than in, so we were glad to get sent here, a normal American place. My boy, Scott, is in Little League and my girl, Susan, is a cheerleader." She smiled with pride and Dale nodded and asked how long the family had been back. Tom and I waited.

"I should have warned you. Dad loves to talk to women," said Tom. He sounded resigned. I shrugged.

"This time it isn't taking long," Tom said. "Dad never gets bored when he's talking to a woman. On this vacation, I'm not going to hurry him."

"I'm on vacation, too," I lied. "I don't have to hurry."

We left the museum and followed the printed guide to the older buildings near the bluff.

"Which one was the Custer house?" Dale asked.

I studied the guide. "The Syracuse houses," I said and pointed to a duplex next to The Rookery, an 1832 building that was the oldest one on the post.

"It says, 'The right portion was once the quarters for the post surgeon and has two front doors—the main entrance, and one that led into his office.' The Custers lived here for a few months in eighteen sixty-eight."

"How about that!" Dale exclaimed.

"How about some lunch," Tom prompted.

"We'll see you at the Pizza Hut," said Dale. They got into a well-preserved Crown Victoria, all cream and chrome, and I got into my sauna-hot CRX. Pizza Hut started in Wichita and no Kansas town is without one.

Nice garrulous old man and his son, I thought. Not likely to be slavering rapists or secret serial killers. Especially the old man. His voice was strong, like someone who is going deaf, and he talked a blue streak, but he had started to look a little pale around the mouth before the son could get him to quit. This was too soon after my dad died. Did I want to worry about Dale? The son was protective and resigned and I recognized a caretaker.

Son Tom—tanned and fit, with deeply set blue-gray eyes the color of faded denim—had scarred hands with scraped knuckles and heavy shoulders, like a blue-collar worker. He looked about thirty-five and was shorter than the old man, almost stocky, and wore the Kansas City suburban uniform: Wranglers, a polo shirt, and running shoes.

He was okay good-looking, nothing special, and when I looked at him and tried to talk to him, I detected something else, an aura of anger that put me off. Don't get nosy, I warned myself. You've gotten yourself into enough trouble in the past.

Dale had the high color of fair men who spend time in the sun. His beefy shoulders had softened with age and he sported a belly that sagged over his belt buckle. The thinning white hair was long and brushed straight back. He looked big and substantial and his voice boomed easily. Why did I think he wasn't well?

The pizza arrived and we helped ourselves. I bit off the tip of a fresh triangle and was grateful for the franchise restaurant— each one reliably like its brothers. You know whether you like the menu and how much you'll pay. The restrooms are in the same place. The help is unrelentingly cheerful, or unofficially crabby. Pizza Huts all smell like cheese and sauce. I munched pepperoni and thought about Dorothy's pilgrimage to the Emerald City. Today she would click her heels and say, "There's no place like a franchise restaurant. There's no place like a franchise restaurant."

When hunger was partly sated, I observed: "Libbie Custer would rather travel with the army than stay home and worry. Of course, she was very young. A little camping is fun, but eventually I miss indoor plumbing."

The old man wiped his mouth and cleared his throat. "It would be fun to go on one of those caravans they put together. Trail drives—live in wagons and camp every night . . . "

A look of alarm flashed across Tom's face.

". . . but I'm too old for that now," Dale finished.

"You said we'd go like regular tourists this time."

Dale shook his head. "I'd *like* to go on a trail drive, but I have better sense."

I studied the two men. The old one, all blarney and bluster, was really the fragile one of the pair. He noticeably drooped before we got our food—maybe a blood sugar problem? The son was quiet, but he was in charge. His attention wandered when Dale and I got into history details.

"What do you do?" I asked Tom, to include him in the conversation.

He came back from wherever he had gone and said, "I run the computer department at the hospital in Independence. All the billing, insurance, records, that kind of thing."

"That must be very interesting," I said. "Computers are part of my job, too." *Were* part. "Where do you live?"

"Independence. I moved in with Dad after my mother died, a couple of years ago. I didn't want him rattling around in that old house alone."

I wondered if he meant Dale couldn't live alone. Or maybe he just liked it there. I kept getting a whiff of resentment. Tom was patient and affectionate with Dale, but he was ticked about something. I wondered what it was. Once I would have assumed that it was my fault, but we hadn't known each other three hours, so it couldn't be.

"My folks live in Gladstone," I offered, "and I live up north, off Barry Road—pretty quiet and woodsy until the next subdivision goes in."

Tom and I chatted long enough to learn where our areas of computer knowledge overlapped, and shared a few complaints about software. Though Tom began to get a little animated talking about his plans for making changes in his department, I discovered that he became wallpaper as soon as Dale spoke.

"I spent thirty years at the Ford Claycomo Plant," Dale said. "Most of it on the line, but I was a supervisor when I retired."

"When was that?" I asked. He didn't look sixty-five years old, but I'm not good at guessing.

"Just this last year. I could take early retirement, so I did."

I looked at Tom, but he looked away.

"So I finally got Tom to come along on a trip. He knows everything there is to know about Navajos and those other Pueblo Indians. He gets his day after Santa Fe."

"This is a negotiated thing," Tom said, smiling. "He wants to stop for every wheel rut, but it would take two months to get to Santa Fe if we did that. Besides, I want him there in good shape."

"So what are your plans?"

"Major stops, like the forts," said Tom, "but not too many drives up country gravel roads. I get equal time, sort of, in New Mexico."

"I'm planning to take my time," I said. "I'm going to Bent's Fort. Everybody in the Westerners' Posse says it's interesting."

"What are those meetings like?" Dale asked. "I belong to the Civil War Roundtable and I thought about joining Westerners."

"You'd be right at home. Lots of older men. We have dinner and a speaker and I've learned a lot. It's nice to have somebody to talk to about western history."

"Why are you traveling alone?" Dale asked.

I started to get my back up, but then I'd been asking personal questions, too.

"That's none of your business, Dad."

"That's okay," I said. "Nobody I know is a history buff. Not to travel with."

"Pretty thing like you, I'd expect a husband," said Dale.

"Thanks. No husband."

The conversation kind of died. We finished our meal, then Dale said, "We planned on Bent's Fort, too. We're going to Fort Riley yet today, then I want to get as far as Larned, although the fort's visitor center will be closed by the time we get there. What are your plans?"

I hesitated. Did I want to see them at every stop? I didn't know what I was getting into. On the other hand, it was fun talking to Dale. And I enjoyed Tom in a remote, anesthetized way.

Dale pushed his plate back. "There's a couple of motels in Larned, and we've got brochures from the tourist information place."

"I plan to camp, but not the first night," I said.

"You don't camp alone!" Dale cried.

"Sure. Staying in motels is too much like business travel."

"Why, if you were mine, I'd . . . "

"Now, Dad." Tom rested a hand on the old man's arm.

"That's no place for a girl to be alone," said Dale. "Why, you don't know what could happen."

"It's perfectly safe—as long as I stick to state parks or national parks," I argued. "They're full of families with kids and old folks in RVs. It's safer than a lot of neighborhoods in town. I wouldn't camp in Volker Park." At twenty-six I was no girl. I appreciated his concern and resented it.

"But you're out all alone, what if something should happen. Do you carry a gun?"

"I'd probably shoot myself if I did. It's really nice of you to be concerned. But I've camped alone out west and it's perfectly safe. If I feel funny, I pack up and leave. I can always pull into a motel. But it's great being outdoors all night, looking at the Milky Way, which you can't see in the city. And waking up outdoors in the morning. I never watch the sunset all the way to the finish at home. Camping's better than being shut up in a motel that smells like disinfectant. And I don't mind sleeping on the ground."

"Well, I don't know." Dale looked unconvinced, but Tom seemed interested.

"If we keep running into each other, you'll know I'm okay. My mother knows where I'm going, in case she needs to reach me. It's perfectly safe."

I tried not to think of Tom. But I wondered, if he worked in an office with computers, where did those shoulders come from? And the scabs on his knuckles?

"Do you have a hobby?" I asked Tom, partly to change the subject.

"I rebuild cars."

That explained the scabs.

"I taught him everything he knows," Dale boasted. "He tore down a Shelby Mustang when he was sixteen and rebuilt it himself and got it purring. I was really proud of him."

"You weren't so proud of the other stuff in the garage."

"What was that?" I asked.

"Rock group."

"Would I have heard of you?"

"The Englewoods. We played around Kansas City in the eighties. I played lead guitar."

"I'd think they were working on his car, and I'd go out and the noise would make you deaf." Dale shook his head, as if he were hearing it again.

"I've heard of garage bands, but never knew anybody who was in one," I said.

"I don't play anymore," said Tom. "But I still work on cars."

"What are you working on now? One of my cousins is into antique cars."

"Karmann Ghia."

"That's not a Mustang!"

"Beautiful car. It's got a big seventy-three Plymouth motor inside."

"I thought the Ghia would die out. I'm glad people keep them going."

"A lot of them are fiberglass now, with an American engine, but yes." Tom smiled. He had a faraway look. "Beautiful design."

"Well, I guess we better be on our way if we're going to Riley," said Dale.

"That's my high point," I said. "Cavalry museum. Custer house. Actually, I'm tired of Custers, but that's what they call the house open for viewing. I'll probably catch you there," I said. I hedged because I wasn't sure I want to link up with them all the way to Santa Fe.

I said good-bye and we headed for the door. As we left the restaurant, Tom delayed until his father was out of earshot.

"You don't have to go along with this." He held my arm. "Dad has a way of scooping people up whether they want to go or not."

I looked at him and heard what he was saying beneath the words: that I had to set boundaries. I'm not good at setting boundaries. On the other hand, Dale was a sweet old man and I was having a good time and it was kind of nice to know I'd see them again and that someone cared if I camped alone.

"Thanks," I said. "If it starts to bother me, I'll let you know. He's a sketch, as my grandma used to say."

"Don't say I didn't warn you."

"Come on, you two," Dale called from the car. "On to Fort Riley!"

I drove west and watched for the white streaks on the green Flint Hills that told me Fort Riley wasn't far.

CHAPTER TWO
FORT RILEY

~

2000

The last notes of "Gary Owen" died away. The flute lingered in the air. The taped voice intoned the end of the narrative. The history of the Seventh Cavalry ended and I turned away from the diorama.

I didn't get too excited about displays of sabers (edged weapons) and carbines (un-edged weapons?). The variations of McClellan saddles were as mysterious as Tibetan prayer wheels. But I liked the general feeling of mounted soldiers, horses, and Indian wars. I even watched the museum's 1926 film of officers riding over hill, dale, woods, and rimrock and falling into the Fort Riley creeks.

Some people never go near museums, not on vacation, not ever, yet I was traveling hundreds of miles to wander through them silently, read signs, and study artifacts. Maybe it was the peace—museums are always quiet, usually air-conditioned. They make no demands. Everything was arranged according to some perfect plan. Nothing ever moved; nothing was ever out of place. If it was, a tasteful sign apologized. The museums were my channel into history. I didn't need to believe in reincarnation because I could learn what life in the past was like in the library and museum—my time machines.

Maybe it's just escapism. I don't watch soap operas or read romance novels, so I escape into the history stories. They cast a spell. Sometimes I wondered why. I locked onto the women's stories and I didn't even have to suspend disbelief—it all happened.

I cased the gift shop, bought a crossed-sabers pin for Dale, and walked over to the house of yellow stone with the picket fence. A heavy wooden sign proclaimed the Custer House.

I felt sweat drip down my ribs and soak into my waistband. The Kansas wind tousled my hair. I knew I was one of those people who never look as perfect as women in makeup ads—the clean-cut and crisply groomed. I have curly hair, bordering on frizzy, and the remains of childhood freckles. Sun and wind make me look even more "natural." Today I hadn't bothered with makeup at all. It would have melted anyway, and I'd look like Tammy Faye Bakker, weeping for Jesus.

In front of the house was what had once been the parade ground and I tried to imagine troopers on horseback, each company on matching horses—bays, grays, chestnuts. I'd seen tanks and helicopters on the way in from the interstate—quite a different sort of cavalry. Stone houses of the nineteenth-century Officers Row blended with the brick and frame buildings of the modern post. I'd have given anything to see a mounted drill, but the best I'd done were John Ford movies and *They Came to Cordura*, with Gary Cooper suffering and Rita Hayworth smoldering.

I stood in the parlor of the display house and wondered why the velvet settee and the matching chairs were so low—inches lower than the piano bench. To accommodate women's skirts? Wasn't it a struggle to get up? People were smaller then. I tried to imagine 5/8-scale people sitting there.

Through the tall window, I saw Tom drive up and he and Dale got out of the car. I'd left my car in the lot by the museum and walked the block or so. I went back out to the porch.

"I got something for you," I said. I took Dale's bill cap off and pinned the cavalry insignia to the front.

"Here, now," he said, but I knew he was touched.

"Why do you think people still talk about Custer?" I asked him as we moved inside.

He thought for a while, then said, "He went down in a blaze of glory."

"Only that?"

"He was young," Dale added. "People remember when somebody dies too soon. Like Elvis."

Tom tried not to laugh.

"Like Marilyn Monroe," I added.

"And he was fighting for the U. S. of A.—going to wipe out those pesky Indians. The Crow scouts told him there were a whole lot of Lakota waiting and he went ahead anyway." Dale thought a moment. We walked into the downstairs hall where two pictures of the Custers hung. "We remember Custer, who was a terrible officer, court martialed, had the highest rate of desertions from the Seventh Cavalry," Dale continued. "Not Crook, not Hatch, not Grierson—all better commanding officers."

"I think it was the flamboyant way he lived," I said. "Of course, we mostly have Libbie's version. They must have had more photo ops than the president." I nodded at a Fort Hays photograph of Armstrong, Libbie, and his brother Tom on a deck under a big cottonwood. "We have plenty of documentation; newspaper reporters were along every step of the way. George Armstrong Superstar."

"I think people like to remember Custer's luck—he was brave."

"Not much for brains, though. My favorite bit," I said, "was where Libbie describes riding over the prairie with him. He reached over and lifted her from the sidesaddle as they galloped along. She must have felt like she was flying. Then he dropped her back in the saddle and she found the stirrup again."

"Where'd you learn all this stuff, Sis?" Dale sounded like he doubted me.

"Mostly Libbie's memoirs."

"Don't you like Custer?"

"I'm not against him. What woman wouldn't like a man who couldn't be separated from her, took her into the field?"

"Women like attention," Dale agreed.

Tom looked amused.

"The Custers actually lived at the end of this row, but this is the house that's been restored." I studied the large, high-ceilinged rooms. No wonder Libbie said it was spacious. I gave half an ear to the woman wearing an ankle-length skirt who was leading a tour group. I imagined "Custer's set" in the parlor.

Dark-haired Mrs. Custer, vivacious and laughing, poured tea and handed it around. Captain Benteen, sitting across the table, looked uncomfortable. Custer, sprawling dramatically on the sofa, had just insulted Benteen's wartime commander, James Harrison Wilson. The Irishman's mouth tightened into a hard, straight line. His ice-blue eyes went dead. His face turned red. His hand shook when he returned the cup to its saucer. Mrs. Custer saw what had happened and tried to smooth it over. By the fireplace, Nettie Smith chattered with her handsome husband. Benteen barked a few words at Custer, excused himself, and marched out. They would be enemies now and Benteen would be excluded from the Custer coterie.

"In the next room," the tour guide was saying, lifting her skirts as she crossed the threshold into a dining room, "is a table with a setting typical of the late eighteen seventies."

I thought the wife of an officer of the Seventh would have had

Meissen or Limoges, not reproduction Blue Willow. I was a snob. Also, I had learned from the curator of the Grinter House Museum that they never put any artifacts on display that a collector would want to steal—all the items within reach were flawed in some way. The cavalry wives would have found a way to import their china and crystal, cutwork linens, and silver to entertain each other. And they did entertain each other—amateur theatricals, musical events, and hops, those weekly dances with music by the post band. Benteen's life was bleak; his wife didn't join him at Fort Riley, or at any other frontier garrison.

I studied the kitchen, Eliza's domain. The kitchen and the little room off of it were separated from the house then. What kind of relationship did they have, living together—the "Ginnel," the Michigan bride, Custer's brother, Tom, and Eliza, the black woman hired in Virginia during the war?

"Come along, Sis," said Dale.

"Dad, why don't you skip going upstairs?" Tom placed a hand on Dale's arm.

"I've waited a long time to see this," Dale replied.

A long flight of stairs in the central hallway led to bedrooms upstairs. Dale mounted slowly.

Tom looked concerned and followed closely.

"How'd you like to live in this house, Sis?" Dale asked when he had recovered. He studied the imposing bed with the huge, carved headboard, and the fireplace.

"If I had servants, I'd like it," I said. "But if I had to chop the wood and carry it for the fires myself, and carry water a bucket at a time, and cook on an open fire—well, it's a nice place to visit."

"Those women had it rough," Dale admitted, "but they whined all the time."

"They certainly did not!"

"Of course they did. Always bellyaching about servants. They expected it to be like their homes back in the States."

"Why shouldn't they?" I protested. "They were sheltered women who did no heavy work. Eliza did the cooking, not Libbie. They couldn't lift their arms above shoulder height in those dresses."

"They oughta had better sense. Adapt to conditions, the way the men did," Dale insisted.

"They were judged by how well they conformed," I countered. "One generation of army wives taught the next what was expected. But the western posts were a new experience and it was hard to live up to the standards set at eastern posts."

"They had servants we don't have today," Dale said. "They wrote about food, their houses and servants, and how hard they had it, unless they were having a fit about the beautiful landscape."

"But they couldn't write about important things," I said. "It wasn't proper to say you were pregnant. You couldn't admit to the folks back home that you were scared or lonesome. You could admit you were afraid for your husband because he had dangerous duties, but you couldn't admit you lived in constant fear of Indians. You couldn't complain because no woman was there when you delivered your baby or that the army pay didn't arrive on time or was discounted or that your husband drank."

"I never read about any of that," Dale answered.

"No—that's just what I said—they couldn't write about what was really happening. So they wrote about the things they could—travel accommodations or living in a wall tent for two years—and the important things slipped out."

"I still say they made too much of little things."

I started to answer, but didn't. Maybe Dale, as knowledgeable as he was, had never considered what *wasn't* said. I thought of the women, recently married, perhaps marching out of the West Point chapel under crossed sabers, in love with their second lieutenant husbands, getting pregnant, having babies, losing them—all without any family—just the woman, her husband, and her child.

Dale and Tom looked in the second bedroom, then wandered back to the big bedroom. I longed to run my hand over the jacquard spread, feel the rough linen sheet, stroke the cool marble dresser top, and run my fingers over the lacy edge of the doily. The room smelled like old wood and fabric. I imagined it once smelled like bay rum and orange pomander and lavender, with a faint whiff of the chamber pot. Instead of tourists' shuffling feet, the sounds from the kitchen would reach up here, the chatter and cries of children.

"Hey, Sis, are you with us?" Dale's hand on my shoulder brought me back.

"Sometimes I get lost in history time."

The three of us walked slowly down the steps and out onto the veranda. Dale sat on the wooden bench and asked, "Where do you go in history time?"

"I imagine myself back there." I stood, feeling the boards of the porch beneath my feet, feeling the dusty hot breeze, squinting against the afternoon light, coming back to the real world. "I imagine that I'm living here, doing what they did, hearing what they said. Don't you get into it, too?"

"Sure! I just wanted to hear what it was like for you. I think I'm sitting on a McClellan saddle on a cavalry horse, out on that parade ground for morning drill."

"Well, I imagine I'm having tea with Libbie Custer."

"What's that like?"

"Lots of fun. She was great for planning entertainment. And Himself was boyish and fun-loving and they had their own clique here at Fort Riley."

Tom listened, but did not join the conversation.

"The general . . . "

"Only Libbie used that title. It was a brevet title. When he was here, he was a lieutenant colonel."

"The *general* began his Indian-fighting career here."

"He wasn't very successful. He chased Sioux and Cheyenne and they out-maneuvered him all that first year."

"He was a great Indian fighter," Dale insisted.

"If he attacked at dawn, on the Washita, when they were sleeping," I shot back.

"That was good tactics," Dale said.

"Black Kettle was a peaceful chief." I was getting hot under the collar. "Why attack his village?"

Dale's face flushed red.

I was suddenly sick of the Custers—the vainglorious, courageous, and stupid man and the self-serving, gutsy, myth-manufacturing woman.

"Why, Sheridan sent him down there! What could he do?"

I started to snap back, but Tom interrupted.

"What was it like when the Custers were here?" Tom often tried to distract Dale. I thought back over things I had read about their first summer at Fort Riley. The news stories and articles stuck to "facts," but the memoirs always mentioned the wind. It blew more steadily than the winds in wooded eastern venues, was drier, harsher, and stronger. At first I liked it because it blew away the cobwebs in my mind. Then my skin felt drawn taut and I couldn't keep my hair from blowing in my eyes. Did it bother Anna Darrah from Monroe, Michigan?

FORT RILEY
1867

"Libbie, you really oughtn't to tease Lieutenant Weir like that. He's in love with you and you take advantage of it." Anna Darrah poked her needle into the cross-stitch pattern. She and Libbie Custer sat on the deep veranda of the house across from the parade ground at Fort Riley. The porch and trim were green and white, a contrast to the pale stone of the house. They sat on plain straight chairs with their handiwork on a scarred deal table. Libbie moved so often she never had things as nice as she ought, with Armstrong a colonel, thought Anna.

"I've known him forever. He was in Texas with us. Besides, he expects it." Libbie sharpened her red drawing pencil with a tiny knife and scratched again at the image on the heavy paper.

The day was soft, with a faint blue haze on the grass. A fresh breeze gusted and was gone. Spring came quickly and bloomed in 1867. Libbie had warned Anna about the harsh summers and she had brought a supply of cream and glycerin lotion with her to Kansas. She intended to enjoy her stay with the Custers, to find out about army life and perhaps army officers, and never, never be a burden.

"You drop your fan for him to pick up," Anna recounted. "You expect him to bring your tea. He does everything short of carrying your mending basket in his mouth like a dog." Anna giggled at the thought, but Libbie scarcely smiled. She continued working on her sketch. "You are merciless," Anna concluded.

"Anna, you are too hard on me. You've only been in the army, so to speak, since we left Monroe last winter. You don't know all the traditions," Libbie said. She picked up her drawing pad and held it at arm's length.

"I know you pretend you are knights and ladies and chivalry and all that," Anna replied. She tied off one piece of floss and cut another, which she threaded through the big-eyed needle.

"It's harmless. The men delight in doing us favors. When they are in garrison, we make their lives pleasant. If the rules weren't as strict as chivalry, it would never do. Lieutenant Weir is my beau ideal, my Chevalier Bayard, a knight *sans peur et sans reproche*."

"Tom brings you gifts. In Monroe, a married woman does not accept gifts from men not related to her."

"It is Tom's opportunity to think of someone besides himself. Bachelor officers have their little diversions. We exercise our social graces. It keeps Tom Weir's spirits up."

"He has plenty of spirits. From a bottle," said Anna grimly.

"I hope to persuade him to take the pledge," said Libbie. "Autie never touches a drop and he's the better for it. But poor Tom! He is such a splendid person, except for that one failing." Libbie resumed sketching.

True, Anna didn't know all the ins and outs of army customs. Still, there was something calculating about Libbie. Anna wondered if it was because she had lost her mother so young. Or because she had no brothers or sisters to temper her ideas. Libbie toyed with the young officers, and broke their hearts.

Except for Will Cooke.

Lieutenant William W. Cooke, from Canada, who had fought in Virginia with Armstrong, had been very attentive to her, even when the scintillating Libbie held forth. He was so tall, so handsome. His dark eyes spoke volumes. And his whiskers!—the most impressive dundrearies in the regiment—brown, full, and uncut, they hung to his chest. Anna stitched her crosses, scarcely noticing what she did, her mind filled with Will's handsome face and his deep, melodious voice. He was so amusing, so comme il faut. Sometimes she thought Libbie was a little jealous of Will's attentions to her. But Libbie was the "old lady" and married-married-married.

Sometimes Anna wondered if Libbie and Tom Weir were closer than friends. Certainly he was in love with her. Certainly Libbie encouraged him. But Anna was always present whenever the young officers came calling. Tom escorted Libbie on public strolls or they went riding with other officers and officers' wives. There was nothing underhanded.

Anna didn't think there was anything more.

Besides, they were leaving tomorrow for Fort Hays since

General Sherman had given Libbie permission to join Armstrong. Libbie's bags were always packed. Anna had spent half the afternoon packing her small trunk. Will Cooke had been in the field all spring, with Armstrong. If they could all be together at Hays, they would have a merry time.

•

Will Cooke lounged in his folding chair. Dinner was over and the four of them lingered over coffee after Eliza, the Custers' black cook, cleared the table. The quartermaster had generously allowed them three tents, plus a fly to shelter their outdoor meals. Fort Hays was a white canvas city on the banks of Big Creek.

"You were frightened, too, Libbie," Armstrong teased, referring to an earlier storm.

The men wore blue flannel shirts and Will wore Indian-cured buckskin trousers with fringe, a far cry from full dress uniforms. Anna tried to keep her wits, but Will was so handsome, so dashing that she could scarcely think straight.

"I never said a word," Libbie answered.

"We couldn't have heard you with your head under the covers," he said.

"I think it was just wonderful that you tried to tie down the corners of the tent," said Anna. She had never been so frightened in her life, but she wasn't going to let them know it. "I don't know how you slept through it."

"After sleeping without even a piece of canvas for protection, you learn to sleep through anything," Will said. He stroked his extravagant facial hair, a cat grooming its whiskers.

"You've been so brave and intrepid," gushed Anna. She hoped the steady wind hadn't turned her coiffure to frizz. She wanted Will to find her attractive. "Even the fright was exhilarating," Anna lied. "I wouldn't for a moment have wished I were home. How can I repay you, Armstrong, for bringing me out here to a life I like so much?" She also wanted Will to think her stalwart and unflinching so he would propose. Many young women came single to army posts and went home with an engagement ring. Why not her? "Are you never frightened?" she asked him.

"When you have gallant comrades, you can manage," Will answered. He and Armstrong exchanged knowing glances. He plucked a blade of grass and chewed the root. Anna poured coffee into his cup. They dined off of thick army china. Armstrong had shooed away Theodore Davis, the *Harper's* artist, and now he and Libbie held hands. Anna was jealous.

"It is so desolate out here, with few trees and very irregular water," said Libbie. "In your letters, Autie, the sun is always shining and the breeze always blows and you always find a camping spot near a creek."

"We manage," said Armstrong. He stroked Libbie's hand. Libbie could be quite practical, even stern, away from Armstrong, but when he was around she acted helpless.

"Some men like to be on the scout," said Will, implying he was one of those men. "I am never happier than when I'm in the company of men who have shared adversity."

"This company of men had a rowdy party," said Libbie. "After the buffalo hunt."

"Our team won!" boasted Will.

"You girls missed a great feed. The other team kept the total killed a secret," Armstrong complained. "If we had known we needed another buffalo to win . . . "

"You still wouldn't have been able to catch one." Will chuckled. "Never did champagne taste sweeter."

Anna looked at Will. She was losing heart. When he talked about being in the field or hunting, he came alive. When he was with her, he seemed—bored? He said all the proper things, and made love to her with the most charming phrases and small endearing presents. But she never felt she had captured his heart. He never looked at her the way Armstrong—or Lieutenant Weir—looked at Libbie.

Perhaps she should set her cap for another young officer and give up on this tall, comely man.

•

Just before his companies left to stop Sioux and Cheyenne depredations, Armstrong had directed the soldiers to put Libbie's tents on the highest ground possible. It was a rainy spring and Fort Hays was sodden. They had a few boards to put down for floors. Anna guarded her little trunk, making sure it was placed on an improvised rack off the ground. Libbie made fun of her for worrying about clothes when they were living rough, but Anna had gone to considerable trouble to acquire a decent wardrobe and she intended to wear it.

"I want Will to see me at my best," Anna had declared. She studied her curly dark hair in her travel mirror and pinched her cheeks to bring some color.

Libbie scuffed around the tent in army boots while her shoes dried. She never complained for fear she'd be sent back to Fort Riley. She'd put up with anything, including grasshoppers up her skirts, to be with her husband.

After Armstrong left, Libbie should never have persuaded Tom Weir to escort her and Anna for a walk outside the post, but none of the dependents—Mrs. Gibbs and her boys and Libbie and Anna—had been off the post for days because of the threat of Indians, who had tried once to stampede the horses. Sentinels were on constant watch.

The huge orange sun burned hot all the way down to the horizon that evening. The country was flat enough that when they reached the top of a swell, Anna could see around her in all directions as the sun slipped from sight. Then a breeze sprang up and carried the smell of cooling grass and the perfume of wildflowers. Dew fell and dampened their skirts as they strolled with the handsome lieutenant.

Tom's round face and bland good looks were deeply tanned

already this season. His soldierly posture and proper manners gave a manly air to all he did—even carrying Libbie's fan or balancing a teacup. He carried his liquor well, too, Anna thought, scarcely showing how much he had drunk, except for a slight problem keeping his balance or, tonight, a tendency to repeat himself in conversation.

She wondered sometimes if Libbie were playing a role with Tom, like an actress in a play—an angel of mercy, saving him from himself.

They meandered away from the fort of canvas tents, chatting as they walked. Libbie kept wheedling to go a little farther, just a little farther and, of course, Libbie's word was Tom's command. The grass blew in the wind, undulating, hypnotic. Tom could see nothing but Libbie and she could talk of nothing but her Autie. Anna might as well have been invisible. She certainly felt unnecessary.

By the time they turned back, it was so dark they couldn't see the sentinel.

A flash, then the report. A bullet whizzed by her ears! Tom shouted at the women and rushed them to a nearby depression. All three hit the ground face down as shots buzzed overhead. Tom shouted at the guard, but couldn't make himself heard over the shots. Anna was terrified. When she looked, she saw Libbie's face pressed into the grass. Anna shook with fear. The sentinel kept firing.

When at last it was quiet, Tom said, "I'll crawl around and approach the post from the creek side and tell the sentinels along the line to let you in."

"Oh, please take us with you," begged Libbie, clinging to Tom's arm. "Don't leave us out here alone in the dark!"

"You must stay here and stay down. I've put you in enough danger as it is."

"You'll never find us again," she cried.

"That's enough." The adamant tone silenced Libbie. He crept off through the grass.

"Oh, Libbie, I'm too fat. I stick up higher than you," Anna babbled. "I've pulled my skirts as flat as I can."

"Now you want to be slender!" said Libbie.

"Anything to be less...prominent." Anna smelled the bruised grass and damp earth. "Do you think Tom will find us?"

"He had better."

Libbie's voice sounded cool and strong. Wasn't she afraid?

"If no one comes soon," Libbie said, "I'll crawl in anyway and take my chances that the guard is a poor marksman."

"What's that?" Anna's heart stopped at the sounds nearby. "Oh Libbie! I hope it's Tom!"

Anna, naturally, wrote a lengthy letter back to Monroe about her adventure. Everyone there wanted to hear about Libbie. Anna had been her friend since they were pupils at the seminary. She had been a bridesmaid at the wartime wedding and a frequent conduit of news about the Custers. Anna had little to say about herself. Will had returned to the field with a courteous farewell— nothing she could count on.

But curiously, Libbie wrote in detail to Armstrong. Anna thought it strange that she would admit she had disobeyed him and put herself in danger, that she would emphasize Tom's courtesy and resourcefulness, that she would beg to be trusted again, that she promised no more walks beyond the sentinel's line. Anna would have kept her mouth shut, lest she anger a husband less understanding than Armstrong.

On the other hand, Armstrong had written at length of women fawning on him in New York last winter. Maybe Libbie was only getting her own back. Or maybe Libbie thought Armstrong might value her more if he knew other men wanted her. Libbie was too deep for her.

Anna wondered why Libbie had not gotten pregnant yet. She

had stopped riding for almost a year, which Anna thought suspicious, but when she brought the subject up, Libbie said she hoped to have children in the future when they lived a more settled life and closed the subject. Anna noticed Libbie didn't dance at the festivities in St. Louis last Christmas on their way to Fort Riley. Anna and Armstrong's brother joined in the wild romps in the evenings. Shrieks and bellows, hide-and-seek, barricades of furniture, dogs barking and joining the chase, followed by a parade of Libbie and Anna being "toted" about and deposited on a table while the dogs barked and men scrambled like wild Indians, shouting and whooping.

Then quiet descended and all trooped to bed and in the dark Anna could hear voices but not words, rustling and shifting in the beds, and she would muffle her ears with her pillow because it was too painful to hear those intimate and physical exchanges.

Libbie told Anna she was afraid they would be sent back to Fort Riley, so for a week she and Anna occupied themselves in their canvas mansion. Anna would just as soon go back to the comforts of the garrison, but she knew that Libbie would strain her utmost to be with her Autie and the farther west she could stay, the better her chances that he could join her.

Then one night after all had gone to bed, a storm began rolling in with vicious lightning and continuous peals of thunder. Anna lay frightened in her cot. The tents had been well-spaced for privacy and they were too far from the adjacent ones to cry for help to a neighbor. Rain poured in the dark, drumming on the canvas. The wind tried to rip the ropes loose and the tents luffed like sails.

Then Anna heard Tom, along with some other officers, asking if she and Libbie were afraid. "This is turning into a tornado," Tom shouted. Libbie undid the straps that held the tent closed and the men and Eliza came inside. They struggled to refasten the straps. Anna calmed down when she saw Tom. The great expanses of fabric were tearing loose from their ropes and the tarpaulin,

which served as a porch, flapped wildly. One lamp was surrounded
by boxes to keep its flame alive.

Libbie called it a hurricane, but whatever it was, it was a fright-
ful storm. The men piled the boxes and furniture up and put a
zinc-covered board across the wooden hardtack boxes for them
to sleep on. The storm passed and the men promised to return if
need should arise. Eliza left for her own tent and the other two
women returned to damp and cold beds.

They had scarcely fallen asleep when a guard shouted, "The
flood is here!" Anna and Libbie crept out of the tent and saw, by
the flashes of lightning, that the creek, an insignificant trickle
when they went to bed, was bank-high. Only treetops were visible. The creek had risen thirty feet in a few hours. As it crept into
the kitchen tent, Eliza took command and directed soldiers to
remove all the household goods.

Tom and the other officers returned, but the roaring water had
created an island where the women were trapped. Anna heard the
despairing cries of drowning men swept into the tempest. She felt
her heart freeze and she couldn't think. Eliza spotted a man clinging to a tree. The only rope not holding up a tent was her
clothesline. She took it, made a loop, and hollered to him to put
it over his head. She tossed it and he caught it. He couldn't hear
over the rush of the water and the roar of thunder. He looked
dazed and the tree he clung to tipped and fell under the bank.
Libbie and Eliza and Anna heard him bubbling and bellowing.
Libbie shouted, "Grab the rope!" and at last he understood,
grabbed it and swung in a half circle until he hit the bank. They
dragged the gagging, dazed man to firm ground.

He was shaken and wild, his teeth chattering. He could
scarcely walk. Libbie gave directions and Anna fetched one of
Armstrong's shirts; Eliza heated coffee to pour down him, and
Libbie splashed through the water to the Gibbses' tent, where she
got whiskey enough to revive him.

But the storm didn't stop and the creek continued to swell, spreading out like a lake. With Libbie in command, they saved two other men that night. Anna and Libbie rubbed them with red pepper and kept the fire red-hot and talked to them until they warmed up. Eliza grabbed another man as he washed past their tent. Anna was too busy to be scared, until she looked at the turbulent flood. Then she expected to be swept away any minute.

The laundresses' adobes flooded and the women and children were evacuated in a wheel-less wagon bed, pressed into service as a ferryboat. Seven men drowned that night. Anna was glad they saved a few. The next morning Eliza broke up her bunk to build a fire to make breakfast.

Anna had had enough of storms, but the next night Big Creek began to rise again. They had to evacuate.

Tom told Anna she couldn't bring her little trunk with her best clothes.

"I can't leave my things behind!"

"Put on all the outer clothes you can," Libbie ordered.

"They're still wet from last night." Anna held a green silk bodice up and carefully pushed her arm into the damp, resisting sleeve. "Oh, Libbie, what shall we wear tomorrow? Everything we have is wet!"

"We'll wear wet clothes."

"But we'll catch our deaths."

"Anna, don't be a goose. Everybody's clothes are wet. We have no choice."

"I must take my small trunk."

"Forget about your trunk. We'll take what we have on," Libbie said.

"Libbie! All my dresses!" Anna began to weep. "What if we should reach a fort? And I'm still wearing the same gown?"

"Anna!" Libbie was out of patience.

But Anna couldn't stop. Her brain was stuck on this one subject.

"The next fort is eighty miles away and there is only water between here and there," Libbie reminded her.

"Libbie, you don't understand!"

Libbie took a deep breath through pinched nostrils. "Anna, listen closely. Put three dresses on, one on top of the other."

While Anna stood immobile, Tom arrived, picked up Libbie, and carried her through the water to the ambulance. Mrs. Gibbs and her sons were already inside. When he returned for Anna, he found her at the door of the tent with her little trunk.

"Surely you aren't going to bother with clothes at a time like this," he said. "We need room for people."

"I'm not leaving without it." Anna refused to budge without the trunk.

Tom stalked off out of earshot. What he said was lost in the rumble of thunder. Her trunk went with her.

Days ran together. Their ambulance rolled over endless grass. That summer was a continuous ride over wet prairie with Mrs. Gibbs and her sons, usually with Tom Weir in the escort, until they reached the railhead at Fort Harker. There Libbie learned from General Hancock that she wouldn't see Armstrong again that summer.

Eventually, the women returned to Fort Riley, where Libbie said each day had forty-eight hours and where she prayed for letters from her Autie.

•

Tom Weir told them later that Indians had been all around their train on the way back from Fort Hays. If their wagons had been attacked, he would have kept a promise to Armstrong to kill them before they could be captured. Anna couldn't say a word.

Something she didn't understand: Libbie was soft and sweet, clinging and silly when Armstrong was around. Hadn't she proved she truly loved him by traveling across Kansas in blistering heat and living in mud just to be near him? But then she was as cool and authoritative as any general when the floods came. She managed Tom, gave orders to Eliza, and kept people amused in camp. Which was the real Libbie and which were roles she played?

Anna always wondered afterward who sent the letter—anonymously, of course—warning Armstrong to "look after his wife a little closer." Libbie accused her of writing it, but Anna didn't know what she was talking about. Some murmured it was Eliza who got Lieutenant Brewster to write it. Eliza was always protective of Armstrong's interests. Or it could have been Benteen or any of the anti-Custer faction bent on mischief.

When Armstrong got the letter, he told his sleep-fogged commanding officer he was leaving immediately on the train, then he raced 155 miles to Fort Harker, arriving at two in the morning. He exhausted his escort and ruined three good horses. He sent an orderly to waken Weir. Armstrong's face was dust-and-sweat filthy, and mud stained his boots and coat. His merciless pale blue eyes showed no fatigue.

He glared at Weir when the officer shambled into the shelter near the tracks. The train would leave in a few minutes.

"Hello, Armstrong," said Weir. His smile was loose and ingratiating. He was half asleep and half drunk. He had buttoned his tunic wrong and stuffed his nightshirt inside his trousers.

Armstrong pulled a letter out of his shirt. "Stay away from my wife!" His voice rang high and hysterical.

Weir started, realizing this was serious. "But old man, we've been friends . . ."

"This letter says you're no friend!" Armstrong threw down the paper and lunged at Weir, who backed away. His fuddled brain couldn't keep up.

"What—?"

"It says you and Libbie are becoming 'too attached.' What does that mean?"

"I haven't any idea. What are you doing with your saber?" Weir stumbled, then fell to his knees. "Please, you must believe me. No shadow of scandal has fallen on Libbie on my account."

"How about the time you were riding and got separated from the group at Riley?"

"We got lost and it took us a while to find our way back. Mrs. Dalrymple was with us, she can tell you."

The saber whirred, slashing the air over Weir's head.

"You know how people gossip. I love Libbie. No! Not that way. Put that thing down!" Weir started to rise, but the point of the saber found the hollow of his throat. "My God, man. I have never overstepped my place. I am innocent. Libbie is innocent. Anna Darrah has been with her every moment since you left. Please! Libbie is the most honest, straight wife a man could hope for. You are wrong, *evil* to think this of her."

The saber broke the skin and a warm trickle of blood ran inside his shirt.

"We've known each other since Texas, since the war. Where is the trust of all these years?" Weir pleaded.

Weir threw himself at Armstrong's feet, utterly abased. Then he had one last thought: "If you harm me, you'll prove the rumors true. If you love Libbie, believe *me*, not that troublemaking letter." Tom felt snot and saliva drip on the splintering floor of the shelter. The sour whiskey on his breath mixed with the smell of coal and the steaming engine outside.

Weir heard Armstrong sheathe his saber. He looked up and the revolver was back in Armstrong's waistband. He started to rise.

"Leave my wife alone!" Through clenched teeth, his voice thin and high, Armstrong said, "Never speak to her again."

"Of course, of course," babbled Weir.

The engineer blew the whistle and Armstrong strode out of the shelter and entered a passenger car. The train began its slow rhythm and Weir remained on his knees, waiting, until the sound faded into the prairie night.

•

Anna sat in her room, embroidering, that morning of July 19 when she heard the clank of the saber, the quick familiar step on the porch. When Libbie opened the door, there was her Autie. Anna wondered if he came from love or because he suspected Libbie was unfaithful. They had a blissful reunion, then that same day a wire from his commanding officer called him back to Harker immediately to face court martial charges for his actions. He had risked his career to be with Libbie.

Anna stayed with the Custers while Armstrong served his sentence at Fort Leavenworth, then she returned to her home in Monroe. She saw the Custers on their occasional visits to Monroe. Then came the dreadful news in July 1876 of the tragic events at the Little Big Horn.

The town was stunned. Besides Armstrong, his brothers Tom and Boston were killed, along with cousin Harry Armstrong Reed, James Calhoun, and George Yates. Libbie helped plan the memorial service, and later, even though her stepmother worried about her depression, she helped Frederick Whittaker, a dime novelist, write a biography of Armstrong. It was rumored that Libbie was destitute, with no income and burdened with Armstrong's debts.

Libbie looked beautiful in black. Anna thought it brought out the pallor of her complexion, which was recovering from years of dry air and wind at prairie garrisons. Widow's weeds became her dark eyes and graying hair. She had lost weight since she returned, but looked the better for it.

"What are you going to do, now that the book about Armstrong is published?" Anna asked. "Are you going to stay here in Monroe?"

"I must begin my life again," said Libbie. "I must defend Armstrong's memory against those awful things people are saying."

"What will you do?"

"I will go to New York where I can respond effectively to comments Whittaker made about the General."

Anna was puzzled. Hadn't Armstrong been a lieutenant colonel when he died? Hadn't Libbie helped Whittaker with his biography?

"Surely there is some occupation there in charities or perhaps writing that a respectable woman could do. Besides, if I don't protect the General's reputation, the carping of lesser men will tarnish it."

Anna remembered the charges at that court martial. Some of them had been true. Armstrong was not perfection.

Libbie was too deep for her. She knew Libbie loved Armstrong, but there was always some other motive at work under the surface. Anna wondered if Libbie was playing another role. She thought about it as her needle outlined flowers and leaves in bright floss. The playacting of ladies and chevaliers was over. Monroe was dull. Libbie would write a new role: the widow of the glorious hero.

"What a slut!" Tom Jackson exclaimed. "Women haven't changed. You can't trust them."

"You think Libbie was unfaithful, then, not just flirtatious?" I asked.

"Unfaithful, of course. She had the motive, means, and opportunity. They were Victorians, but it's always the same."

"It must be human nature."

"Why can't honesty be human nature? It's just an excuse when you call it that." I wondered what brought that on.

"You got to give him credit, Sis," said Dale, changing the subject. "Custer was one dashing fellow."

"But they were such strange people. Libbie was one minute mocking herself and her artificial hair, and the next minute intrepid and cool-headed in an emergency. Her memoirs give one picture, but the records give another. When she wrote her version of history, she just left things out that didn't fit the myth."

"They were a model couple for the times," Dale asserted.

"He fathered a son on the Cheyenne woman Monahsetah, after the Washita battle."

"There's no proof!" Dale declared.

How many people have to say it? I wanted to argue, then thought better of it. "Weir's cause of death was 'melancholia,' probably a euphemism for advanced alcoholism."

"You must've read stuff I never read," said Dale, sounding annoyed.

I shrugged and got up from the bench. Dale looked away, but Tom's eyes danced and I thought he might have smiled. I waved good-bye and got in my oven-hot car.

∾

From the porch of the Custer House Tom heard a few cars and trucks on the local roads, plus a fainter noise from I-70. The mid-day heat had silenced birds. The chatter of the departing visitors faded.

He stifled impatience at Dale's slow shuffle. He wondered if Dale were weary or if he wanted to prolong the moment. When they reached the car at last, Tom cranked the AC up to high and waited for his dad to settle himself.

"Maybe we could drive around a little before we hit the inter-state," Dale said. "I can sorta see what this place must have looked like back then."

Tom steered the Vic down the street with the yellow stone Victorian houses, and then tooled through the post. The buildings got newer as they headed back to the highway.

"Why are you dragging that woman into our vacation?" Tom growled, then added a fake chuckle so it wouldn't seem like a serious question. He raised his voice over the blast of cool air and the hum of the motor.

"Why, I think she's interesting. She knows her history. Told a crackerjack story I hadn't heard about the Custers."

"This was going to be just the two of us." Tom realized he sounded childish. Why did Dale have to talk to every woman he met?

"We're shut up in the car together for hours. I like a little break from you, Son, much as I'm glad to go with you on this trip."

Tom tried to remember a time before his mother died, when everything was "normal" and his father "behaved." Something happened after she died. At first Dale sat. Didn't even turn the TV on, just looked at the blank screen. Then he went to church or the senior center and all the widows played up to him. And he started going out more. Then he gradually became The Man Who Loved Women and they poured out their hearts to him. Tom squelched a tremor of jealousy. He found it difficult to talk to women. How could he trust them? At least it got Dale out of the house after he retired. It wasn't as though Dale didn't revere the memory of his mother. He dusted all her knickknacks carefully each week and put them back in place. Tom couldn't get him to pack up her clothes and send them to Goodwill yet. Dale still had an air of sadness when he was alone.

"Why did you start talking to women?" Tom asked as they raced past Junction City exits.

"Where did that come from?" Dale asked.

"I was wondering why you started talking to every woman. When, or why, or what you get out of it."

Dale thought while the still-green Flint Hills rolled by, then he said, "You remember Eppie?"

"That crony of Mom's?"

"Yes. She lost her husband, cancer, about the time your mother died."

Tom heard a choke in Dale's voice when he said "your mother."

"Sure."

"Well, we were at a meeting at church. Prayer meeting, stewardship, something, and I started to tell her how sorry I was about Rupert and I got tears in my eyes and stopped. Then she said, go ahead, she still cried every time she remembered he was gone. And we both cried a minute."

Dale stopped, then made another effort to explain. "I saw in her eyes the same pain I felt."

Dale stopped and Tom considered what he had said. Then he said, "What about Carla? She's cracking jokes and going off into her history stories."

"How often do you run into somebody with the same hobby?"

"Are we going to spend our whole vacation with her?"

"Not if you don't want to, but I did ask her to meet us for dinner in Larned. Don't want to be rude."

Tom had to be satisfied with that.

∾

I aimed the CRX into the sun all afternoon, stopping in Abilene for gas and a glass of iced tea in a restaurant, but I skipped the Eisenhower Museum. I never watched the sky change through the sunset unless I was driving. The changing sky pulled me west. It was higher and wider.

Kansas advertised its great tourist attractions tongue-in-cheek: the world's largest ball of twine, the world's deepest hand-dug well, the Museum of Independent Telephony. The state tourism people bribed visitors one summer: stay twenty-four hours, visit an approved attraction, eat a large meal, stay at a motel, and you will get a Coleman cooler. Most people kept driving, getting to Denver in one day, but I loved the landscape and the wide horizons.

Maybe the pursuit of history was a new religion. I got spaced out, did my devotions, and achieved a temporary tranquility. It was a strange interpretation of "religion" but if you think the goal of worship is serenity and a sense of your place in the universe, then history is mine.

That story about Weir and Custer and Libbie always made me wonder. What was going on? Anna Darrah, called "Diana" in one of Libbie's books, is funny and naive. What hanky panky could go on with all those people around? Maybe Himself had been unfaithful and so could imagine Libbie unfaithful. Unhappy Benteen probably sent the letter. He survived the Little Big Horn, but alcohol eventually claimed him.

Even someone mythic, like Custer, could feel what everyone feels. Envy is a cold core of nausea in a hot shell, the misery of loving someone hopelessly, without reason or stint, unstoppably—and knowing he doesn't love you. Or doesn't love you as much, or quite the same way. What did I do when it happened to me? I just hung on, hoping I was mistaken. Then Kevin left. I blocked those memories. I'd think about Alice Grierson, a solid, motherly presence, whose experience at Fort Riley was very different and yet much the same. Libbie had never known married life outside the army, but Alice Grierson had been an Illinois matron before the war. When they were at Fort Riley Ben Grierson was commanding officer of the Buffalo Soldiers, who would move south and west in the next decade. And Alice had another baby.

I fought the memories that crept into the blank hours of driving and ran like hamsters on a wheel. I listened to public radio, changing stations as I drove out of range. Somewhere south of the interstate, on 156, I gave up and let the tears run—for all the mistakes and things I should have done and the losses. I steered one-handed and blew my nose.

Would it have been easier not to have children, like the Custers? What would have happened if I hadn't gotten pregnant?

Was it a punishment for my sins? Bad karma? Why take Antonia, the blameless joy of my life? There were no answers. I could only drive through the ripe summer fields, implacably silent. The stars gave no answers either, but turned inexorably in the sky. The sun shone and the wind blew and I was a piece of dust blowing westward.

I loved the rolling countryside—the fields of wheat and corn spacing quarter sections between woods and creeks, the neat farm buildings, and the browsing cattle. But I did wish it didn't take so many hours to get from one fort to the next. By the time I got to Larned I was flaky from watching the road. I checked into the biggest motel and changed into a swimsuit immediately and hit the little pool, logging short, steady laps for half an hour. After I showered and dressed, I went outside, where I found Dale sitting beside the pool, ready for dinner.

CHAPTER THREE
FORT LARNED

❧

$\mathcal{D}$ale, Tom, and I walked across the highway to the Sunset Cafe. Dale insisted on holding the door for me, of course. The restaurant was a pleasant, homey place with a counter and tables and booths. Three waitresses in white shirts and black slacks moved efficiently from kitchen to customers with heaping plates.

Tom and Dale indicated a vacant booth, but I liked a chair with a hard back after sitting in the car all day. We took a table near the back window. The dinner hour was winding down, with customers bidding the waitresses good night.

Our waitress displayed a plastic tag that said "Morgan."

"Are you ready to order or do you need some more time, Hon?" she asked as she placed glasses of ice water and silverware rolled in a paper napkin at each place. She pulled an order book out of her apron pocket.

"Give us a minute, sweetheart," said Dale. He smiled at her.

"Did you enjoy your swim?" asked Tom.

"Always," I said. I was aware that my hair was still damp. If it didn't dry looking okay, I'd probably never get in a pool, but I had naturally curly hair (naturally frizzy, most of the time), so I didn't have to set it or fuss with a drier. I hadn't bothered with makeup, either. After all, I was on vacation—no e-mails, no messages, no briefcase, no Franklin Planner, no heels, no tailored dress with padded shoulders.

"Did you take some time out?" I asked.

"I got Dale to put his feet up while he watched the news." Tom looked calm, as always. I wondered if he ever broke a sweat. I wondered what rattled him.

Dale was watching the waitress, whose black pants were snug across the hips.

I wondered at the elderly man's ability to charm every woman he met. He had a friendly, almost courtly manner and I would bet that most women assumed, because of his age, that he was harmless.

We ordered steaks and settled back to wait.

"Well, it's been years and I'd forgotten how much fun it was to crawl around those museums and see all that stuff," said Dale. "I've got pictures of all the cavalry gear, every book there is, I think. But it's not the same as seeing the real thing."

"I don't even know the names for the parts of a saddle, but looking at one with those slits makes it real," I said. "Weren't they awfully uncomfortable?"

"Easier on the horse, though," Dale said.

"Not a single mention of a woman in the Fort Riley museum—not a drawing, not a photograph, not an artifact. Then they had three shelves of books by and about army wives down in the gift shop."

Dale shrugged. "Is that where you bought my saber pin?"

"Maybe," I said.

"That just suited me right down to the ground," said Dale. "I'd never buy something like that for myself."

The way he said it made me glad I'd thought of it. Just a little thing, but Dale appreciated it. I settled back against my chair, feeling pleased. I was relaxed from my laps in the motel pool and I would be completely content as soon as I got something to eat.

"Your steaks will be right along," Morgan announced as she passed our table. She bused two tables and carried the bus tray to the kitchen. The next time she returned, she had our dinners.

I had never liked soft rolls as much as crusty Italian bread and the curious salad bar had a big bowl of iceberg lettuce and a bowl of homegrown cucumbers, followed by containers of macaroni salad, potato salad, cottage cheese, watermelon, and chunks of what looked like bread pudding—not my idea of "salad." The steak was perfect, though—charred almost black on the outside, dripping pink on the inside, and fork-tender. I sighed and began.

Morgan came by to ask if everything was all right and it was. Later she checked to see if we wanted desert. "Y'all traveling?" she asked in the friendly way of small-town people.

"Going down the Santa Fe Trail," Dale announced.

"We get rut nuts in here quite a bit in the summer," Morgan said.

So that's what the locals call us.

Dale put his fork down. "You from around here?" he asked.

"No, I'm from Wyoming, but I ended up here so I can see my daughter now and then. She's in Lawrence at the university."

"You look like you've had an interesting life," said Dale. His eyes twinkled and it was obvious he enjoyed Morgan.

Morgan looked forty and had a couple of bad teeth, but was pretty in a quiet way, and seemed competent. "Is that like, 'May you live in interesting times'?" she said.

"Sometimes that's how it seems," Dale agreed. "Why don't you join us? If you're through for the day."

Morgan got herself a cup of coffee and pulled a chair from a nearby table.

"Tell me the most interesting thing about your life lately," Dale said. To my ears, he seemed to be offering his attention, not demanding anything.

Morgan hesitated, then said, "You don't want to hear about my troubles."

"Not unless you want to tell them." Dale waited.

"If y'all would like, I'll show you the wheel ruts, before it gets dark," Morgan offered.

"I'd like that," Dale said.

When we finished eating, Morgan took off her apron, spoke to the cook, then walked outside to a clean Mitsubishi pickup; Tom got in with her and I drove Dale in my car. Morgan led us past the Trails Center and Fort Larned, both closed for the day. I turned down one road, turned and turned again on a gravel road, and drove past a tidy farm, past machinery parked in front of a red barn, past neatly mowed lawn surrounding the house, which was guarded by windbreak pines.

I pulled into a fenced parking area with a Park Service sign. Fifty feet away in a field stood a raised wooden observation platform. I walked the mowed path, heard chittering in the grass. A hawk rose from a fence post, swerved and swooped overhead, then found another fence post and watched us.

I pulled the dark dried heart of a blown sunflower off the stem. This was a bushy species with dozens of small yellow blossoms, not the kind with one huge flower. Sticky sap oozed on my hand and when I sniffed, I was surprised at the resin smell, like pinesap.

The flat farmland was beautiful. Clouds gathered color for a spectacular sunset. The earth exhaled the rich loamy smell of the fields. Then I realized what was strange: except for birdsong and the whisper of the wind, it was silent. No traffic, no city hum, no motors or machinery. I could hear the small sounds. Far away a piece of farm machinery clanked briefly, then stopped, and the peace came back.

I loved the smell of tawny summer grass. The huge sun turned the clouds pink, lavender, and mauve against the Wedgwood sky. I climbed the observation platform, built of oiled four-by-fours. From the ten-foot advantage, I could see prairie dog holes. The noise in the grass must be prairie dogs. The dying sun threw the depressions of the wagon ruts into shadow. Tom's deep-set eyes disappeared in shadow. Morgan shaded her eyes with one hand. Dale studied the trail ruts intently, before following me down from the platform. I wore sandals, not a good choice for walking through grass where twisty little cactus grew. We found the weathered ruts, and I stepped into one. It was like meeting a person you had only read about. Dale walked across the wavy ruts, back and forth, back and forth. Morgan and Tom waited.

I wanted to lie down and feel the ruts with my body, but I was too embarrassed. Instead I bent and pressed my hands to the dry and cracked earth. The brittle grass waved. The flat little cactus was a dull green that made it almost invisible.

The sun slipped below the horizon as we walked back to the parking area. Morgan chatted with Dale, who made her laugh.

"You kids go on along," said Dale. "I'll see you later."

"You can't do that." Tom looked grim.

"The lady and I want to continue our conversation," said Dale firmly. He looked his son in the eye.

"You need your rest. You can't go running around 'til all hours. You hardly know her. You don't know..." Since Morgan was in car shot Tom didn't specify what.

"Morgan will drive me to the motel later." Dale walked over to the pickup and climbed in the passenger side. I could see Morgan talking, then Dale shook his head. Morgan put the truck in gear and backed out of the parking area.

"Will he be okay?" I asked.

Tom shrugged. He was still glowering.

"You have lots of patience with Dale up to a point. Then this set you off," I observed. We got in my car and headed back to town, sailing through well-kept fields and past neat farmhouses. A hawk traced curves in the sky. An irrigator sprinkler dribbled water from its aluminum pipe.

"He's foolish about women," Tom said. "And not very discriminating. I can only do so much."

"Morgan looked all right."

"You can't trust women." Tom stared straight ahead. I saw the ligament in his jaw flex.

Outside my motel room I asked, "Does he do that very often?"

"More times than I can remember. He would always talk to anybody and since my mother died, he talks to women. I think he's lonesome."

"So is that waitress."

"Well, they're both adults and he's a good listener," Tom conceded.

"He never offends. I don't understand how he does it."

"Me neither. I'm not that outgoing. He offers and lets them decide how much to respond."

"It's incredible."

"It worked for you."

That stopped me. "Yes, I guess it did." Tom waited while I struggled with the key. The lock was hot from the day's heat and reluctant.

"What's your agenda for tomorrow?" he asked.

"Fort Larned, of course, since we're here. It opens at eight, and there's a visitor center. Then Dodge City."

"You going to get into a Custer brawl again?" Tom grinned.

"I'll try to behave myself," I answered. "Dale seemed surprised at stuff I take for granted."

"It's been a while since he read most of that history and he hasn't kept up with the newer books."

"He's probably forgotten more than I'll ever learn."

"Sometimes he gets confused," Tom reassured me. "Besides, he's not used to a woman's spin on the story."

"This has been a good day," I declared. "I enjoyed your company and Dale's. I'll catch you at Fort Larned." And I went inside.

I undressed and wondered why I didn't care about Tom. Once, I'd have been my most flirtatious, trying to please, big eyes and hanging onto each word. But now . . . didn't care. Didn't care that I didn't care.

Tom's face came to mind easily. I tried to imagine lying in the trail ruts with him, making love and listening to the prairie dogs' chatter. But the fantasy machine had shut down. Didn't care.

∾

Morgan told Dale about her daughter, Dorene, who was majoring in engineering at Kansas University, on the drive back to town.

"You like a cold beer?" she asked as she drove past a tavern on the main drag.

"I don't do that anymore," Dale said, patting his chest. "Is there any place we can go and just talk?"

"I've got a pitcher of iced tea in my refrigerator and some chairs on my patio. Why don't we go to my house and I can take my shoes off."

Dale agreed and Morgan drove to a small house on a side street. A tortoise-shell cat greeted them and wove eights around Morgan's ankles. She excused herself and disappeared into a bedroom, sending out a huff of perfume when she closed the door behind her. Dale studied the little things she had done to the house—potted plants in the windows and framed photographs on the end tables, notes and snapshots and fliers stuck on the fridge. Fruit in a wire basket on the kitchen counter. A clean tablecloth on the kitchen table. He wondered if he could ever learn to do those little things that made a place homey. He hadn't changed anything since his wife died. He dusted the china dogs and had the doilies washed. He kept the framed photographs on the mantel, her sewing basket near her chair in front of the TV. Tom urged him to get rid of some of her knickknacks and clear her clothes out of the closets, but he couldn't bring himself to do it yet. Or maybe do it ever.

Morgan came out wearing pink fuzzy scuffs. Dale followed her into the kitchen, where she squeezed lemon and stirred sugar into tall glasses of cold tea and carried them out the back door to a concrete patio.

Dale sat in the slick white resin chair and looked at the tidy yard in the last of the evening's light. Morgan lit a citronella candle in a glass container and the smell brought back a thousand summer nights when people used to go outdoors after dinner to cool off. The concrete under their chairs was still warm from the day's sun. Morgan must have cut the grass that morning—cut blades were still green and the smell of zoysia was familiar.

"You're a friendly man," Morgan said. She pulled another chair over and put her feet up.

"You looked like you had a story to tell."

"Well, you're right about that. I've worn out everybody around here, telling it over and over. I can't seem to quit talking about Billy, like that's the way to rub away the memories. I thought they'd fade by now, but I still cry when I think of him." The last words came out funny and she pulled a tissue out of her pocket and covered her eyes until she could take a deep breath.

"Why should you care?" she asked.

"Why not?" Dale smiled benevolently. "It's a free country. I like to listen to women talk."

"Well, okay, but if you get bored with it, I'll stop."

Dale waved his hand for her to begin.

"I was doing okay before Billy came along, so I'll be all right again," Morgan said. She looked at Dale to see if he believed her.

"I'll get used to Billy being gone," Morgan continued. "I

mean, I've got friends and I'm talking to you right now, but I won't say I haven't cried some hard tears."

"Talk it out, sweetheart," said Dale.

"I get dressed for the lunch shift and I know this is just a waitress uniform, but I have somewhere to go and something to do when I put it on." Morgan smoothed the front of her white shirt.

"My trouble is I liked cowboys, back in Sheridan where I used to live in Wyoming. I waited tables there, raised my daughter. My husband was a cowboy, worked at a ranch up by Dayton. If I'd known he was a drinking man, I wouldn't've married him, but when we were head over heels in love, he was sober all the time. He started drinking the next winter when we were shut up in that house trailer. I can always stay busy, but he couldn't stand to be indoors and you can imagine what the winters are like, not that we have an easy winter here."

Morgan looked into the distance. She was no longer on a Kansas patio. She was back in Wyoming.

"We were together long enough for him to get fed up and me to get Dorene, my daughter. I've worked hard and raised her right and she's at the university here in Kansas. She's smarter than me. She's waiting tables to put herself through engineering school, but she won't be waiting tables forever."

"You don't look old enough to have a kid in college," said Dale gallantly.

"I got an early start. Besides, you know what they say—it ain't the age, it's the wear and tear."

"Is she why you moved?" asked Dale.

"I had to get away after Billy left. Billy is a good man and I don't regret a thing, although he didn't have to call names. I could've called him a few."

"Where did you meet him?"

❧ ✦ ❧

Well, I like the rodeo, used to go every chance I got. I went to the professional ones out of town and the local ones at the fairgrounds. Me and my girlfriend were sitting in the stands, drinking a beer, watching the events. Just last August—it seems like a lifetime. The crowds at the rodeos in Sheridan are usually in a good mood, and they have somebody on the PA announcing events and cracking jokes.

There's that tension, waiting for the man to nod, then the cowboy and the horse leap out of the chute. On steer roping, the steer jumps out and the roper leaps after him, twirling his loop, pigging string in his mouth, and he can't come out too soon and he has to tie all four legs and they have to stay tied six seconds. It's fast and dangerous.

The first night of the county fair, I noticed this cowboy. I was in the infield bleachers so I could see better. I caught him looking at me. I smiled and gave him a thumbs-up sign. And when it was his turn for steer roping, he took his hat off and looked right at me before he set his chin and gave them the nod to let the steer out. I was real touched he noticed me.

It was the county rodeo and people were standing around the chutes and when Billy got finished, he came over and said, "Don't you work at the Stockman's Cafe?" and we started talking.

I've seen a million cowboys just like him, even here in Kansas. They've all got faded shirts and sun-scorched hair. They've got pink cheeks over a deep tan and clear eyes and tight little buns in their Levi's. That was Billy. And cute. He had big blue eyes and a straight nose and he could've modeled western clothes for a magazine.

We went out after the rodeo that night. He's younger than me, and not just in years. He was thirty, but more innocent than Dorene.

He said, "You're good luck, Morgan. I did real good today. Made my entry fee back and then some."

I said, "Glad to hear it." We had a couple of beers and he acted wary at first.

"How come you were watching me?" he asked, both big hands wrapped around a longneck Budweiser. It got noisier and noisier at the Bozeman Inn as more cowboys came in from the rodeo. One even had his number still safety-pinned to his back. The Little Joe band pounded out another song and I leaned toward Billy so I wouldn't have to shout.

"You looked so determined."

"I was concentrating," he said.

"Even in the stands, I could feel the tension."

"It's all hard and tense and I have to focus on one thing."

"That sounds like something else," I teased.

It took a second, then he ducked his head and grinned.

"I usually do okay," he said.

"Are you single?" I asked.

He took offense. "I wouldn't've asked you if I wasn't."

"Just checking. I'd think a cute guy like you'd have a girl." I saw a flicker of something hurting in his eyes, like a cloud's shadow across a mountain.

"I've had girls," he said.

He looked at me real close. I'm no *girl*.

"Why fool around with an old lady like me?"

"You looked like you were having a good time," he said. "I like a woman with a nice sense of humor." After a couple of beers Billy loosened up and told stories about the ranch where he worked and the only way I knew he'd been drinking was this wide, canary-eating grin. We danced in front of the cold fireplace until the band quit.

He was a perfect gentleman, only gave me a little kiss when he took me home.

I went back to the rodeo the next day, of course. He found me between events and we talked.

Billy was okay at steer roping but he had a good horse for that. What he was really good at was steer wrestling. Before I cared who he was, I noticed he just slid out of the saddle and had his arm under the steer's right horn and his heels dug in the dirt in one smooth move. Then his left hand grabbed the other horn and twisted the bull's nose into his front pocket. Before you knew it the steer was down with his feet off the ground and Billy was walking away slapping dirt off his jeans. It takes a big man to twist a steer's head and get him down. Some of those ranch kids missed their steers altogether or danced them around for as much as a minute before they gave up or the steer got away. Some big guys aren't fast enough or coordinated. Billy was, every time.

I admit I was the one who really started things. The first night it was a peck on the cheek and the second time when he walked me to the door, I grabbed him before he could walk away and gave him a kiss I hoped he'd remember. "For good luck," I said. Then he kissed me back and he was like a drowning man—it was mouth-to-mouth resuscitation. We went inside and he was thirsty every which way.

Now I don't go with just any man. I never wanted to show Dorene a bad example. I've had boyfriends, but I'm not promiscuous. I was pretty stuck on Billy.

When I looked in Billy's eyes I felt dizzy, like I'd lost my balance, and his face was beautiful. I didn't say "Stop." He woke up three or four times that night and I, uh, gave him resuscitation. Neither one of us talked much the next morning. He went back to his motel to get changed without saying five words.

That Sunday afternoon I went to the infield and waited for his events. He looked tired, but he grinned when he caught my eye.

It was a set-up steer, one that tried to climb the gate. And it stopped twenty feet out. Billy almost missed it and went down off balance, his timing just a little off. I heard him grunt when he landed and he must have fallen on the horns. He couldn't get a grip and the steer twisted and then Billy was flat on the ground.

My heart stuck in my throat and then they were grabbing me because I was trying to get in the ambulance. They wouldn't let me in because I wasn't family. I ran to my car and drove to the hospital. I felt like Delilah and I'd cut Samson's hair and it was my fault he'd gotten hurt. They set his dislocated shoulder and taped his broken ribs and I took him home in my car because I couldn't stand to think of him hurt like that with nobody to look after him.

Well, he stayed with me three weeks and I brought him meals from the restaurant. Not really nursed him, just babied him a little. He was grouchy and grateful and sweet and cranky. We made love anyway, very carefully, like porcupines. Don't tell me cowboys aren't tough.

It felt kind of good to be taking care of somebody again. Maybe I thought deep down he'd stay if I took good enough care of him. Then one morning before I left for the lunch shift he said, "I entered up at Billings."

"You're still all taped up!"

"I'll be okay."

"You'll end up crippled."

"I can't live off you like a kept man forever."

"It ain't been forever yet!"

He was standing at the kitchen counter making a peanut butter sandwich. His hair was standing up in back and he looked about fourteen years old.

"I don't want you to go." I was trying not to cry.

"I gotta go."

"Haven't I been good to you?"

"Yes, and I'm obliged."

"Then stay."

"I can't," he said. "I don't like playing around with somebody I'm not married to."

"You knew that the first night when you came inside." I was real hurt by that.

"I couldn't help it," he said.

"Then why'd you do it?"

"I got carried away. What I do and what I think is right when I calm down ain't the same."

"But I did it for you. How do you think that makes me feel?"

"I just can't stay with a woman who sleeps around."

"That's not fair. You're making it seem dirty."

"You're choking me down. I can't say the things you expect and you're hurt because I don't and it's harder than ever to say them."

"What things? Like 'I love you'?"

He nodded.

"Hasn't anybody said them to you before?" I asked.

"Yes, but after what happened, I can't believe them."

"What happened?"

He took a bite of his sandwich, then he couldn't swallow and he had to get a drink of water, so he put the sandwich on a plate.

"I had this girl in Billings. I thought she was my girl, anyway, but she had lots of boyfriends I didn't know about and when she got pregnant, she said it was mine. And I'd have to pay child support."

"That's awful." That cooled me down a bunch.

"I had to get a lawyer and she never would give any blood for a test, so finally she married another guy and had the baby. I mean I feel sorry for the kid, but she was taking advantage of me."

I listened.

"I drank a lot, waiting that out," he said. "I was working on a freight dock all day, to make money to pay the lawyer and maybe pay her to have the baby, I didn't know. Then I remembered my dad coming home drunk when I was little and I decided I wasn't going to be like him, even if my luck turned bad. So when it was settled, I went to this big ranch and stayed out of trouble, away from town mostly, until now. I thought I'd try rodeoing, just to see if I was good enough."

"Let me make it up to you," I pleaded.

He shook his head. "You're smothering me."

That hurt so bad I couldn't say anything. I had to go to work and when I got home that night he'd cleared out. There was a note under a vase with a dozen red roses. "Thanks, Morgan. You're the biggest-hearted woman I ever knew.—Billy."

I felt like I'd saved a man from drowning and after he was okay, he said he didn't like people who do lifesaving.

Pretty soon I'll forget the way his hair curled around his ears and how he looked at me. I won't think of his breath on my neck. I moved here so I can see Dorene. The folks here are real nice. This bad time won't last forever.

⤚ ❀ ⤙

Morgan tried to stop her tears. Dale stood up and gestured to her, so she stood up, too. "Let it go, sweetheart." He put his arms around her.

She sobbed and sobbed. She wailed and gasped, wiped her face, and sobbed again, chest heaving. Dale could feel Morgan shudder, feel her chest heave, feel her crying—wet and convulsive and knotted—without getting torn up by it. She needed somebody in case she couldn't stop. Finally, she slowed down, coughed with a dry sound and swallowed several times. She wiped tears, blew her nose, then blotted her face on her shirtsleeve.

They both sat back down.

"You needed to do that," Dale said. "Now you need to say, 'Billy and I will never have that again,' and let it go."

"Billy and I will never have that again," Morgan repeated. And again, thoughtfully, then she said, "I hate to give up even the bad feelings. They're all I got left."

"What do they get you?" Dale asked gently.

Morgan was silent. "You're probably right."

They sat in the dark, and the stars grew brighter. Even with the streetlights, Dale could see the Milky Way—never visible in city skies. An occasional car rolled by. A mother called Brian home. They finished their iced tea.

"Will you be okay?" Dale asked.

"I think so," Morgan answered. "Do you want me to take you to the motel?"

"No hurry," he said. He reached over and she put her hand in his and they sat together in the soft summer night.

෴

The officers' row at Fort Larned stood at right angles to the visitors' center, separated by a rolling stretch of green grass. Dale and Tom and I had walked around the buildings, and Dale pointed out reconstruction, cleverly done, which I wouldn't have noticed. After a while the heat drove us into the shade of the Quartermaster Storehouse, which stood open and empty except for stacked boxes of pristine wood and a few other props.

We had stopped at the Santa Fe Trails Center, then driven past the state mental facility where signs warned us not to pick up hitchhikers. We had watched the film in the visitors' center and looked at the exhibits. I wished they would only put items found at Fort Larned in the Fort Larned museum and not bring in things from other places just to complete a display.

The barracks had been furnished in 1860s style, with double bunks. It seemed strange for two adult males to share a bed, but it was common then. Now I knew the original meaning of "bunkie." The barracks were perfectly furnished with authentic reproductions or originals of the furniture used. The sergeant's room featured artfully arranged cavalry accoutrements and a desk for paperwork. Clear plastic over the doorway kept visitors out.

It looked like a movie set. Everything was perfect and it was obvious that it had never been used. The raw floor planks were still pale and clean. The blankets had never been slept in. The rifles in the rack looked as though they had never been loaded, carried, or fired. It was all accurate; it looked fake. When the Park Service took over the site, only the walls were standing. The "barracks" had been used as a barn. The Park Service re-did everything, but no troopers ever lived in that room.

Dale, Tom, and I wandered around the square of the parade ground, behind the shops building where wagons stood, into the reconstructed blockhouse, which was an interesting, six-sided fortress, never used since Plains Indians preferred raids and guerilla tactics and would never attack such a well-defended position, if they could help it. The original octagonal blockhouse had been dismantled for its stone. All the interiors had to be reconstructed except the officer's house open for display.

I was beginning to droop and it was only 10 A.M.

"Getting tired, Sis?" Dale asked. He looked a little flushed himself.

"Sort of. I need something to drink. I've got a cooler in the car. We can have a soda in the picnic area before we leave."

"Sounds good. Do you want to do that now?" Dale treated me like a sweet little thing. Since my dad had died, nobody treated me like that. It made me feel cared-for. It made me aware that I'd never have that father's affection again.

"Going strong, Dad?" Tom asked.

"Strong enough," said the old man.

A beautiful young woman, whom even the Park Service uniform couldn't make unattractive, unlocked the building at the end of officer's row and a group of six tourists entered the furnished house. Dale, Tom, and I quickly followed to hear what she had to say. The design of the building was similar to the one at Fort Riley—a sort of duplex, with two living units under one roof, separated by a thick wall. The stone was gray-black, not the warm tan of Riley. The two sides of the building shared a well and a neat fence enclosed the backyards. I tried to imagine ranking out—where a higher-ranking officer and his family got the best house and created a domino effect, causing each family in turn to move to smaller quarters. All army wives complained. The army must not have had enough budget to house its people. Mrs. Orsemus Boyd had to move five days after giving birth to her third child, and then she, her husband, and children lived in a single room.

The room at the front of this Fort Larned house once housed an officer, his wife, and infant, according to the sign.

"I don't know how they did it," I said.

"What's that, Sis?"

"I guess if someone else does the cooking somewhere else and you take the dirty clothes to the laundress, you could live in one room. But she must have been constantly tidying up."

Tom read the notice, then nodded. "Crowded quarters."

Dale followed the Parkie and the other visitors outside, but Tom and I stayed behind.

I studied the cradle at the foot of the curving sleigh bed. I had read about but never before seen a stenciled carpet of lengths of canvas sewn together, then tacked over straw to keep nails in the rough floors from pulling the hems out of dresses and petticoats.

"I wonder what she used for a diaper pail," I said. "Babies need many changes of clothes, too. I bet even then they had boxes of toys—handmade dolls and animals and blocks and toy carts, all over the place. Where are they?"

"This isn't authentic enough for you?" Tom teased.

"This is the best house I've seen," I said. "Look at that antler hat rack—they must have done that. They have pegs on the walls, that's a nice touch. All the stuff on the mantel and on those shelves. I think that's a hair wreath in that big frame over there."

"I can hear a 'but' in your voice." Tom bent over the fence that kept visitors at the door to the room and looked more closely.

"But as cluttered as they made it, when three people were living in this room, it must have been overflowing with stuff. Those women wore at least three petticoats. Where did they keep all their clothes, their husband's dress and undress and field uniforms? They couldn't keep clothes, baby gear, everything in one dresser."

"You're not getting lost in history time," Tom said. "Have they left out too much, the way the women left things out of their letters?"

I looked at Tom. "You've been paying attention. Those women were usually newlyweds, young and sheltered," I said. "They had to travel a long way, first on the railroad, then by stage or army ambulance or spring wagon, like that one we saw in Leavenworth. Then they got to a bleak army post—Fort Larned had no trees back then. The Indians burned the prairie grass every year. It must have looked like the back of the moon to them."

"Why did they come? Why did they stay?" Tom asked.

"They loved their husbands, they said," I answered. "They lived in crowded rooms, or dusty adobes. Mrs. Boyd lived in tents for two years in Nevada and Arizona. Later they said they missed it."

I looked at the "doctor's rooms" with their stuffed birds and mounted heads and cases of instruments. Curios like the basket made of shells and the silver dish for calling cards caught my eye.

"Once the average young wife got to a post she had to get used to no fresh milk or no vegetables except what she grew. Then she would get pregnant. Out here, with only a contract doctor at a small post like this one, the woman must have been terrified. No mother, no sisters or cousins or aunts to answer questions."

"Or make it worse with old wives' tales," Tom said.

"Maybe. But women of that time supported each other. They passed on the morality and the family stories and gossip and instruction. Back home, they would help sew the baby clothes, sew Mother Hubbards for her, comfort her, make over her, reassure her.

"Some of the young wives were lucky. If the post was bigger, other officers' wives would be there to help her. They had had children and could tell her what to expect and be on hand when the time came. Helen Singleton was all alone. No women's voices. That must have been very hard—no voices to comfort her."

I walked to the bachelor's room with the buffalo rug on the floor and sabers on the wall, hunting rifles stacked in the corner. The compartmented desk spilled paper. An antelope skin covered the narrow bed.

"What happened to Helen Singleton?" Tom asked.

"She wrote a diary, not meant to be read by her family or anybody. She wrote her fears—would the baby be normal? Would the delivery go smoothly?—all the things any woman worries about. Then in pauses the day she was in labor, she focused on writing a sentence or two, to take her mind off the pain. Some of it is almost surreal." I thought about all the stories I had read. The women, in letters or memoirs or diaries, always talked about the wind. Even today it was tossing the trees along the river and rattling the corn in the fields nearby. I needed a hat to keep my hair out of my face. It made me a little edgy that it always blew so steadily.

FORT SANDY
1872
Thursday reveille
Cassius was assigned to this post and he loves me and
I love him and I don't imagine living away from him,
but oh! coming to Ft. Sandy is different for him. I
dote on him, but sometimes that isn't enough. He is
beginning his career, testing himself, proving himself,
but this is not a natural break in a woman's life. I prove

myself by making a home and rearing children. I
despair! Everything I learned from my mother about
how to be a good wife is impossible here. The cold
creeps through the cracks in the wall like a ghost.
Dust smothers everything. I try to make this room
cozy for Cassius, but it is a melange of odd furniture,
a washday stew of all our things, jumbled together.

Fold your clothes and clear away the dishes.

If I am ill afterward, who will care for the baby? If I die,
there is not even a minister to read the prayers. Oh,
Heavenly Father, please help me through this.

I smell smoke. Is the fire out?

Where is my mother, telling me what to do? I could hear
the women if I concentrated: Mother's contralto, Aunt
Jessie's twitter. The broken arpeggios of the girl cousins'
laughter.
     My grandmother's voice. I can still hear the song of
her voice—not anything in particular she had might
have said, like "A stitch in time saves nine" or "Pretty
is as pretty does"—just the soft tone and the high pitch
and the march of her words.

Thursday noon
Which call was that? The bugle tells the time.

Women's voices in the kitchen, or talking over the
stutter of the sewing machines, talking under the July
trees at church socials. Women fanning themselves,
watching the children play.

I'm so hot today.

Thursday stables
I learned nursing and preserving and disciplining
children. Sew a fine seam. Keep your husband's
interest, or avoid it. What to use.

How does Aunt Mabel put up her cucumber pickles?
Is that heat rash or poison ivy? A woman's place is
with her husband, even if her mama has more money.
    Whither thou goest, Cassius.
    What happened to that Cozak cousin who left for
the gold fields in '49?

Thursday taps
We all knew Bess was a harlot, but her Aunt Rose took
her in, and said she wouldn't treat her blood kin that
way. Then the baby died.

Use it up, wear it out, make it do. It's what you do with
it. Now she's paying the price. She wasn't any better
than she should be. Her husband's wishes.

I want this baby to come. Why does it hurt so much?

"What happened?" asked Tom. "Was she okay?"
"The diary just stops. She had the baby. I don't know if she was
sick or just busy afterward. Later, she started making entries
when she found time, but she never was that candid again. She
never threw away what she wrote that one long day, though."
    We walked outside and found Dale just outside the big open
hallway chatting up the young Parkie. The woman, who had a

long blond braid twisted up in back, managed to look appealing. Dale must have turned on the charm because the girl smiled and her eyes were alive and I heard her say something about a degree from the state university.

"There you are, Sis," said Dale. He introduced me to the Parkie and I smiled. Traveling with Dale held interesting surprises. "Where'd you say to go for lunch?" he asked the Parkie.

"Freddy's, on the main drag in Dodge City, just past the museum and tourist things."

"We were going to have a cold drink before we leave. Why don't you join us, if you won't get in trouble?" Dale said. The Parkie looked at her watch and said, "I'll tell them inside."

We collected some sodas from my car and walked across the bridge over the Pawnee River to the picnic area, where a middle-aged man sat writing in a notebook. A 35mm camera and a roll of film sat in front of him. Something seemed out of place. I looked around and saw the Jacksons' Vic, but no other vehicle.

"How'd you get here?" I asked, sitting at the table. I offered him a soft drink.

"Walked," said the man, who introduced himself as Dick Brown from Kansas City. He was fortyish, tan and fit, and wore a vest with bulging pockets.

"From where?" asked Dale.

"About ten miles down the road." Brown explained he was walking the Santa Fe Trail—backward. "I drive my old van to where I want to stay tonight, then I walk back to where I started and get my Dart." He told us about his van, with the stove and bunk, and the people he met. "Last time I was in Santa Fe, I was on crutches. My leg didn't want to heal from 'Nam in seventy-one. I vowed the next time, I'd walk. My great-grandfather was a drover, a cowboy, and there's a lot of family history connected with this part of the country." After a few minutes, he began his eastward trek to Larned and we all wished him luck. He had the look in his eyes, I thought, of a man who was, however temporarily, free from routine.

I spread my map on the picnic table and weighted it with my Coke. I showed them where I planned to camp that night, at John Martin Reservoir east of Bent's Fort.

"After I leave Dodge City, I'll go straight to the campground at Lake Hasty, set up my tent, and get settled. You're staying at that motel at the turn-off, so I'll catch up with you at Bent's Fort the next morning."

"I still don't like the idea of you out there all by yourself." Dale frowned and I felt a replay of all the discussions I had had with my mother.

I gave him my standard reassurances. "It's perfectly safe. Families go to state parks. Church groups. Retired people. I'll be fine and I'm looking forward to sleeping outdoors."

"Let's have breakfast at the La Junta motel at the turnoff to Bent's Fort tomorrow, so I know I don't have to call the state troopers out to find you," Dale insisted.

I was touched that he cared, but exasperated. "How about eight?" I said and looked at Tom, who maintained a studiously neutral expression. "Are you getting bored?"

Tom started to lie, then shrugged. "All these forts start to look alike after a while."

"They are alike," I said. "There's actually only one fort and the national park people reproduce it. They have a forts manufacturing plant at Yosemite, hidden deep inside Half Dome. It's all fiberglass, stamped out with molds. Like Disneyland. Then they truck the prefab units to a place in the middle of nowhere. They do the same one at each site."

The pretty Parkie nodded in solemn agreement. "We have to take an oath never to tell. If we do, we get sent somewhere where we have to do the same talk three times a day all summer with no time off. Parkie madness!"

Then Tom caught on and laughed and Dale said, "They had you going there for a minute, didn't they?" and Tom had to admit we had. The Parkie enjoyed the joke.

When I waved good-bye on my way out of the parking lot, Dale was still talking to the Parkie, who laughed and answered him. Tom looked amused.

∾

Most people from Kansas City treat the state of Kansas as a five-hundred-mile delay for western vacations. I had driven west many times and had come to think of it as a day's meditation on prairie, wheat, sky, and grass. Kansas was a geographical division, but it was also a clear break between regular life and vacation. I kept a bottle of water beside me on the car seat and drank steadily, then had to pee steadily. Which was easy on the interstate, but harder when I drove the two-lanes. I needed to stop more often than I needed gas, so I bought snacks and fruit juice at convenience stores. Now, on this second day, I still checked my watch. Except for my rendezvous with the Jacksons, nothing was scheduled. The campgrounds stayed open, the creeks kept running, the lakes weren't drained at five. I only had to think of time if I wanted to get into visitor centers.

The army posts marked time with bugle calls and kept a firm routine. The post returns were a bare record of daily business on army posts. The doctors' reports on weather and civilians treated and epidemics gave a different view of daily life in the garrisons. The doctors recorded the weather and many were amateur naturalists, collecting plant and animal specimens. When historians added the wives' memoirs to these records, a fuller picture emerged.

I thought about Helen Singleton's diary, which wasn't typical. Usually the diaries and letters were written for posterity or for the people back home. Occasionally the truth slipped out. I tried to

imagine what the women would have said if there had been no
social pressure or genteel manners.

General Sherman encouraged the wives to record their experiences and they did in literate and restrained diaries and letters,
which are vivid and immediate, as first-person narratives often
are. Some of the stories are heartbreaking. Little Edith Grierson
died of typhoid fever just after her thirteenth birthday. Newly
widowed and pregnant Mrs. Fetterman was forced to leave Fort
Phil Kearney in a blizzard. Jim Bridger led the ambulance filled
with other widows and children to Fort Casper through a storm
that froze troopers to death in the saddle.

The memoirs written years later were cheerier. Mrs. Summerhayes described her naked Indian butler serving dinner. Mrs. Roe
enjoyed fishing and hunting. Libbie described the larks and
jokes. They remembered the friends and parties and especially riding in the breathtaking landscapes. Charles King's sentimental
novels of garrison life softened memories further.

Why did they fascinate me? If I had ancestors who had lived on
the frontier like the trail-walker, Dick Brown, I could understand
my interest. Men must fight and test themselves and women
must weep and wait. Their voices spoke to me. Maybe I'd write
my own memoirs and in thirty years I'd look back on a vanished
time and remember the good parts.

∾

Dale tarried until the pretty Parkie had to go back to work. Tom
wanted to hit the road, wanted to hurry. Dale learned all about
her classes, her professors, her roommates, and her boyfriend.
Tom made himself take a breath and remember: this was a holiday. They didn't have a schedule, except to get to Bent's Fort by
tonight. They had plenty of time.

Hawks or turkey buzzards wheeled in the sky. The climbing
sun bleached the blue sky and tan fields. They smelled skunk

roadkill and almost missed a turn, but once they were on the two-lane to Dodge City, Tom asked: "Why did you go with that woman last night? You didn't know her from Adam. She might have—" but he couldn't think what harm she might have done. After all, she had been kind enough to show them the wheel ruts.

Dale smiled. "She had a story to tell."

"Why do you have to be the one to listen? I mean, I don't care, it's a free country, but I never know what you'll do next."

"You don't have to worry about me."

"You had one heart attack already."

"Talking to women keeps my heart warm and pumping."

"After Mom died, after you had your heart attack, you started going to all the senior center events, talking to all the women."

Dale nodded. "That's right."

"Well, I was just glad you had something you liked to do. Better'n sitting around the house."

"I thought I could do some good. Not like a doctor or somebody like that, like a minister, just like a friend. I'm so old they don't suspect any hidden motives. I'm so old, I'm harmless." He chuckled. "I don't want anything, except to listen to them, so they tell their stories and I get to hear them. It's a privilege to hear them tell me all about their lives."

"It can't always be that interesting."

"It is. The women are interesting. I get to see how other people live and think and feel. Whole education."

"I wonder what Carla's story is."

"She's a deep one. But there's something there. She's a little too jumpy, a little too ready to joke or tell a story. What did you two talk about at the Larned house?"

"She commented on how cold the rooms looked, too neat, not like real people lived in them. She even got me into the story, a little."

"Then she and the Parkie got you with the fiberglass forts. That was good!" Dale laughed again.

Tom ducked his head in embarrassment. He didn't say anything. He knew he should lighten up; it was only a joke.

"Let me know when you need to stop. We're off the interstate and there're no rest stops."

"I'll give you plenty of warning."

Wheat fields almost ready to cut waved in the constant wind. Farmhouses might be scrubby or lavish, usually with four-wheelers and pickups parked in the yard. The empty Kansas roads stretched ahead.

CHAPTER FOUR
DODGE CITY

∾

I felt ratty by the time I found Freddy's in Dodge City. It was almost two and my blood sugar was rock bottom. I missed the restaurant the first time and was all the way out of town before I knew it. I drove back and found it the second time.

The Jacksons were not there. I had driven through the real Fort Dodge, now a veterans' hospital and retirement center at the edge of town, which made me late, but Tom and Dale were running later. Probably still talking to the Parkie. I wasn't going to wait.

I ordered a steak and filled a bowl at the salad bar. This one had raw vegetables. I would be too grouchy if I waited any longer. As I ate I thought about all the things that affected my personality that I couldn't tell people: low blood sugar, today's complaint, which made me shaky; PMS, which made me hyper and extremely short-tempered; cramps, which made me distracted. These were not subjects for polite dinner conversation with casual acquaintances. Other woes that really bothered me and made me short, tense, or hard to live with: tight shoes; cold sores; sitting too long, which makes my back hurt; binding elastic when a bra shifts; a muscle cramp on one side of my neck when I'm tense. That started after a fender-bender whiplash. When it hit, the spasm was so acute I couldn't think straight. I had collapsed with heat exhaustion shopping in the dry, deceptive Tucson heat one afternoon and now too much heat wiped me out.

These were easily remedied and not serious, but I reacted as though they were life threatening.

At least once on every trip I found myself miserable, frightened, and weeping. At that moment, I always wondered why I went anywhere, and especially, why I went alone. It was only the second day of this trip, but I was already feeling short with the world and ready to complain. One more museum was my limit.

This wasn't what I wanted to feel. I knew I couldn't fight what had happened and I couldn't be happy.

∾

Once they arrived, Dale and I talked about the "real" Dodge City and the fort, which was once a few miles out of town.

"I passed it coming into town. It's a VA hospital now, but you can still see where the parade ground was and there are a few old houses and a church." I sipped coffee.

"Maybe we'll double back and see it," Dale said and looked to Tom, who nodded.

When we finished eating, we drove both cars to the historical area. The gift shop and ice cream shop and the restaurant and the staged gunfight in Front Street for tourists supported a serious museum, the Boot Hill, in Dodge City.

"I'll get the car and drive you up the hill, Dad," Tom suggested.

We were standing by the ticket booth at the Boot Hill Museum. We would have to climb stairs to get to the displays.

"I can make it," Dale insisted.

I eyed the long, steep flight of steps doubtfully.

"I can phone upstairs and they'll let you in the side door," the ticket seller offered.

"No, I can make it," said Dale stubbornly.

I wished I could say something funny to lighten the mood. It wasn't really my responsibility, but my solar plexus knotted when Dale and Tom disagreed.

"You'll have more energy later if we drive up now," Tom said. He nodded to the ticket seller, took their tickets, and walked toward the car door. Dale had no choice but to follow.

I climbed the stairs and took deep breaths, willing the knot to relax. Dale entered the upper level of the museum from the outside and mumbled something about Tom parking the car. He caught up with us in a few minutes and the three of us wandered around the exhibits upstairs. I was impressed and hadn't expected to be. One display featured dozens of photographs of nineteenth-century citizens of Dodge City. As we walked through the exhibits, Dale chatted up the guard—a woman in a period cotton dress and sunbonnet. Then we made our way down the stairs.

"Rough folks," I said. "I didn't see any of them packing a gun except the lawman."

"No. Is that so?"

"Reality was a lot different from Matt Dillon and Chester."

The rough wood stairs seemed steep and I grabbed the splintery rail. Dale usually did all right coming downstairs, but I noticed he was very slow. Maybe he had reached his museum limit, too.

The museum continued at street level behind the period storefronts, which looked like a movie set.

Lunch had raised my spirits and blood sugar briefly, but I was fading again. Dale sat on one of the benches.

"Do you want to wait here for the gunfight?" Tom asked.

"I just want to sit for a minute," said the old man.

I saw that his color was bad. "You stay out too late honky-tonking last night?"

He patted my hand. "Don't I wish!"

Tom scowled. Hadn't he caught on that my first defense was a joke? This reminded me too much of what happened last winter with my dad. I remembered without wanting to. I was in the living room of my parents' house. Snow covered the ground and the blinds were shut against the glare.

"I used to have lots of guys asking me out, Pop," I had said. Papa Tony was tilted back in his Naugahyde recliner, staring at the picture that flickered on the silent TV screen. He looked gray and his voice had no strength. It was a week before the final heart attack.

"They see you're still raw and bleeding," Papa had said. "Give yourself a chance to heal."

"It's been a year. I'll be old and gray soon. Nobody'll look at me."

"Treat yourself kindly."

"How do I do that?" I had asked.

"Treat yourself the way you treat your friends," he had said. He looked at me, sitting on the edge of the couch, and smiled. "You wouldn't put them down or condemn them or give them a hard time. Lighten up on yourself."

So here in Dodge City, I was trying. I was taking myself on a nice trip and showing myself a good time. And I was worrying about a sick old man again.

"If you like, I'll get the car," Tom offered.

"Since I'm already here, I might as well look at the stuff. This is better than I expected." He stood and looked around. He had a wooden cane I hadn't noticed him using before.

"I thought this was just *Gunsmoke* tourist stuff," I said, "but the museum goes down to the ice cream shop. And there's that house at the end. I wonder if that's Miss Kitty's house."

"You're too young to remember that," said Dale.

"Does the word 'syndicated' ring a bell?"

"Of course. I taped a bunch of those shows," he said.

Dale and I entered the museum. I was thankful for the air conditioning. Tom followed, watching Dale and not paying much attention to the exhibits. I was tired and didn't feel like talking.

"No Women in the West lecture?" Tom asked after a while.

"No, unless you want a fast minute or two on Squirrel Tooth Alice." The display window mannequin dressed in period clothes tilted sideways on her chair. "Look at her photograph."

"What's that blur?" Dale asked as he studied the photograph.

"Her pet prairie dog," I answered.

"I wonder where 'Squirrel Tooth' came from?" mused Dale. "She's a fine-looking woman."

"Maybe when she grins, her front teeth stick out," I suggested. In the photograph, a curly-haired woman dressed in a velvet dress appliquéd with flowers sat in a chair covered with a fringed throw. She wore a jet necklace and ear bobs. She looked as respectable as a preacher's wife, with a steady gaze and calm expression.

"She was one of the early doves in Dodge," I said. "Probably set up business when the fort opened. A lot of the Kansas prostitutes had business names. I've seen photographs of 'Timberline' and 'Cotton Tail.' They operated without a pimp or bordello, out of tents or cribs. Adventurous girls would 'light out for the territories,' too. Huck Finn wasn't the only one. Most of the girls were in business a couple of years, and then they married and became respectable wives and mothers. Coyote ate Alice's prairie dog, though."

"She looks so sober," said Dale.

"They had to hold a pose a long time for a picture, and a smile starts to wobble. Everybody on that picture wall looks sober, but I've read about the jokes they pulled and I think they probably laughed a lot."

"You tell us history stories about these women, but you never tell us much about yourself," said Tom.

"You haven't told me why you're so down on women," I countered.

"Bad experience. With a woman, of course. What about you?"

I didn't want to talk about myself. I wondered if Tom *wanted* to learn more about me, or was just being polite. "My life is boring," I answered. "The history stories are interesting." I could tell them about myself, tell my own stories, but they were too painful and I'd just met these people. Besides, I was afraid if I did tell the truth, they wouldn't like me. And I did like hanging out with Dale and talking about history that nobody else I knew cared about.

A woman sewed a Folklore-pattern dress in the dry goods store. I didn't want to interact with the living history exhibits. I nodded and kept on walking. At the print shop Dale turned and said, "We'll see you at breakfast."

This seemed abrupt. "Are you feeling all right?"

"Just a little tired," Dale reassured me. "I'm ready to sit in the car."

Tom looked worried, so I felt upset. "Is there anything I can do? Do you want to stay here for the night?"

"Don't make a fuss," Dale said. His voice had an edge and I wished I had told him about my father, so he would understand.

"If you say so. I hope you feel okay. I'm going through the rest of the exhibits, and then I'll drive to Lake Hasty. I hope it isn't raining when I get there."

"Do you camp in the rain, Sis?"

"Not if I can help it, but I've got a good tent."

"If you were mine—" he began.

"She's not," Tom said.

"I've got to say something." Dale turned to me. "You're a woman alone. You don't have any weapon to defend yourself. Anybody could come up and take advantage of you." Dale sounded upset, as well as angry.

"Most of the time," I answered, trying to be patient, "there are kids and bikes and families in RVs and people on honeymoons. Most people camping have a live-and-let-live attitude—

don't bother them and they don't bother you. I've been amazed that I could leave my camping gear all day and come back to find it all there."

"I just don't think. . . ."

Tom shook his head and Dale stopped. I wanted to scream. I was tired and only compulsive museum trotting kept me going. I knew Dale pushed my buttons and he couldn't help it.

"I appreciate that you care," I said. I kept the anger out of my voice.

Tom left to bring the car down the hill. I gave Dale another short lecture on naughty ladies on the frontier and we discussed whether the *High Times* miniseries was accurate with its row of prostitute's canvas tents in a mud street in the movie's recreated Dodge City.

"There's a story I probably don't know enough about to tell," I said. The steamy day enervated me. I could imagine thousands of steers kicking up smelly dust a few miles away at the processing plants. I could imagine the plains wind blowing pollen from millions of wheat plants. Dale looked tired, but Tom looked impervious to heat, wind, or fatigue.

"Is this another story about a woman?" Dale asked. He wiped his forehead with his handkerchief, and then swiped the back of his neck.

"It's a story about a young, handsome—they're always handsome—anyway, an attractive lieutenant transferred here. I got some information from the post returns."

"I've heard of those but I never read 'em."

"Reports, daily and weekly, by different officers—who was present, on detail, or sick. The army surgeon recorded hospital and sick call information, weather, and some scientific things."

"Sounds boring."

"It is, unless I'm looking for something, then it's a paper chase and I'm a detective. This lieutenant, Nathaniel Joseph, was transferred here from Fort Concho. I found out about him by accident when I was reading about Grierson and the Tenth Cavalry in Texas, then I found his name on the post returns at Fort Dodge when he arrived. For some reason, I remembered his name."

"The forts moved west and south as we pushed the Indians back," Dale offered. I nodded.

"I picked up a little there, then some more when I was reading about buffalo hunters in Dodge City. The fort, as you saw driving into town, was about five miles from where the town was then. See that line of dying cottonwoods over there? That's where the river used to be, not practically at our feet."

〜 ✦ 〜

His West Point graduation photograph depicts Lieutenant Nathaniel Joseph's huge, melting dark eyes and regular features. When he departed from Fort Concho in 1870, he left behind a scandal about a young woman in San Angelo town.

By the time he arrived at Fort Dodge, he was about thirty, with an independent income, a silent Indian servant, and a reputation as a womanizer.

The post returns give the skeleton of the story. Nothing is heard from him for a time. The local Dodge City newspaper reports altercations between buffalo hunters, gandys from the lengthening Santa Fe railroad tracks, and the troopers from nearby Fort Dodge. The buffalo hide market was at its peak with hides stacked fifteen feet high for half a mile beside the tracks. Each group thought it owned the town. The post returns offer scanty details. A letter from his commanding officer to his wife revealed Lieutenant Joseph had "ruined" several women at Fort Gibson and Fort Leavenworth.

This could mean a kiss that wasn't followed by a proposal of marriage or actual intercourse. A private conversation between a young man and woman was called "making love." It's hard to tell.

Lieutenant Joseph was comme il faut with flawless manners. He was a prized dancing partner at the weekly Friday hops.

One chilly day early that spring Lieutenant Joseph escorted Anne Egan, daughter of the commanding officer, into town for some shopping. They ran into Tom Nixon, who was at the rail terminal bargaining with a buyer for buffalo hides.

Nixon turned and eyed Miss Egan. "Nice day," he said. His eyes ran down her figure.

Lieutenant Joseph scowled. Anne tightened her grip on his arm, nodded, and they continued toward the dry goods store.

"I don't like the way he looked at you," Lieutenant Joseph growled.

"It's nothing," Anne replied.

∾

In Dodge City that spring, a drunken buffalo skinner killed an inoffensive Negro, a former soldier who ran errands from the fort to town. The hidemen wanted to lynch the skinner, but he escaped. Rumors started that the army was going to take over the town, or burn it to the ground. The hunters and skinners were ready to battle the army.

Tom Nixon visited the hidemen's camps, spread a half-mile around the town, swearing that they were a match for any soldiers. Nixon, with his sunburned and wind-dried face and thinning red hair, once killed 2,600 buffalo in twenty-four days. He could hit a fly at one hundred yards. His reputation for toughness was well known. The hidemen readied their rifles and Sharps .50 buffalo guns.

A few days later, on a cool spring night, the officers' wives put on a masquerade at the fort. Officers' wives, children, and guests dressed in costume. At a frontier garrison like Fort Dodge people made their own amusements. Young women and children appeared in a pantomime and the army orchestra filled the meeting hall with music. The austere room had been draped with bunting and butterfly milkweed and blue wild indigo brightened the buffet table. After the entertainment, the young ladies changed and couples danced until about eleven, when the orchestra ended the gavotte with a flourish. Quiet conversations filled the room as couples gathered at the tables for a collation of roast beef, pickles, and summer vegetables and lemon custard. Men in undress uniforms and white gloves gave their arms to women in décolleté evening dresses with silk or taffeta skirts pulled into bustles. The evening had cooled, but the dancers' cheeks showed their exertion.

Captain Januarius Egan, the commanding officer of Fort Dodge, stepped up to the platform where the army musicians rested.

"My dear friends," he began. He beamed at the assembly. Conversations stopped and everyone turned toward him.

"My friends, Mrs. Egan and I are happy to announce the engagement of our only daughter, Anne"—he looked at his daughter with a father's loving pride—"to Lieutenant Nathaniel Joseph." Everyone clapped, although a few young women didn't look happy.

The young couple glided in front of Egan and bowed and smiled. Captain Egan whispered something to the band conductor and the orchestra broke into a waltz. Lieutenant Joseph and Anne Egan turned in graceful swirls around the room while the audience watched. Anne's pale skin showed a pink flush. Her eyebrows were black as ravens' wings, as was her curly hair, and her lips pouted rosy. Yards of bluebell silk covered her slight form. The style was out of date, but here on the frontier it didn't matter. Lieutenant Joseph leaned close to her, seeming to need to breathe the same air as she did. His dark hair thinned a little at the temples, but his body was taut and muscular. He moved with grace through the steps of the waltz. She seemed to emit golden light and he seemed her shadow.

Captain Egan led his wife to a chair and sat beside her, beaming at his daughter and her future husband. After the waltz, the orchestra played a polka and the couples' dancing resumed.

"D'you think he'll be good to our Anne?" asked Mrs. Egan. She surreptitiously blotted a tear. She was plump as a pouter pigeon with pink cheeks and white hair. She held an idle ivory fan. Egan was short and feisty, used to giving orders and having them obeyed. His bald pate shone. He had the high color associated with short-tempered people.

"He'll answer to me if he doesn't." Egan was known for his quick temper and prompt action. "There, there, lovey. It had to come one day. She's a headstrong girl and needs a firm hand."

"But Lieutenant Joseph's reputation."

"We won't heed any gossip." Egan looked around the room with satisfaction. The post ran smoothly, for the most part. He'd lost his brevet rank of colonel after the war, but he was the commanding office of this garrison. His officers were steady men and the new second lieutenants were coming along.

"Shall we go, my dear?" he asked, leaning toward his wife.

"Yes, please. It's been a long day."

•

Later that evening, Anne Egan allowed herself to lean against Nathaniel's chest. She smelled tobacco smoke and male sweat in the scratchy woolen tunic. Nathaniel bent his head near hers, attentive. She sighed.

"Are you weary?" he asked.

She could almost feel the deep resonance of his voice through the shoulder of his coat.

"A little."

"Shall I escort you home, my dearest?"

"Not yet. I don't want to leave you. My heart is beating fast just because I am near you. We are truly engaged. We can set the date anytime. It has happened so quickly."

"Not quickly enough." He brushed her temple with his lips. "I long to hold you with a husband's care. I long to cherish your body as though it were my own. I want your beauty to enfold me. How long must we wait?"

Anne shook her head. "My love," she murmured.

"Come." He led her from the meeting room. The breeze cooled her damp face and chest. Nathaniel pulled her shawl up over her bare shoulders. He laid a gentle finger on the cameo she wore on a velvet ribbon around her neck, his engagement present to her.

He drew her gently across the parade ground. Barracks, corrals, offices, and housing all stood at strict right angles. The parade ground showed faint rippling where it had been raked. A quarter moon shone down on the gravel. He stopped beneath the flag, which leapt and snapped on its standard. The prairie wind wrapped Anne's skirts against her legs.

"When, my love? I cannot wait. Let us seal our pledge." He kissed her softly. Her arms flew around his neck.

"We mustn't!" Her voice, full of longing, undercut the meaning of the words.

"Tonight."

"Oh no."

"Yes." He kissed her and his probing tongue unloosed sensations new and dangerous. He cupped one breast, lifted it free of the bodice, bent, and lapped the nipple. Anne swayed and felt her knees give way. He ran his hands down her sides, held her upright, then lifted her from the ground. He fastened his lips on hers and they turned slowly, slowly under the tossing flag.

An hour later, Anne heard his footsteps outside her bedroom door, as arranged. She had left the front door unlocked and now he was here. She froze in fear and excitement. She felt the air in the room move as he pushed the door open. She couldn't breathe.

His knee bumped the side of her bed. She gasped, felt him locating her, touching her, kissing her, pushing her nightgown up her thighs.

"My love." His breath mixed with hers. "I worship you. Give yourself to me."

•

Sometime close to morning, Captain Egan got up when he heard a prowler. His wife breathed quietly beside him. He didn't want to disturb her, so he got up without a word. Their quarters were two-story. His bare feet trod the creaking boards of the rough wood floor. Cool air billowed his nightshirt and chilled his bare skin. His shoulder brushed the rough plaster of the wall. Faint sounds of horses reached him from across the parade ground. He heard footsteps.

The intruder was escaping! Egan hurried down the stairs. There was bright moonlight on this clear night, but no light inside the house. The intruder pulled the hood of a wide cloak down over his face. Egan drew his saber from its sheath and felt the gold cord swing against his leg.

The intruder stopped and turned, recognizing that steely sound. He stumbled to the fireplace, picked up a poker, and struck at Egan. Egan gasped when the poker found his shoulder. He nearly dropped his saber. The intruder slashed toward him. The fight was clumsy, without enough light. Egan cried out, "Stop, sir!" then the prowler lunged at him. Egan thrust and the effort threw him off balance and he fell, crashing against the fireplace fender. His head hit one andiron with the sound of a ripe melon bursting.

The intruder escaped.

Anne, who said she had been awakened by the noise, found Egan's body almost immediately, according to the inquest record in the post returns. She was hysterical and given a sedative by the post surgeon. The killer was never identified.

The next Sunday Lieutenant Joseph sent food and wine from his own stock for an enlisted man's wedding. He joined the party, where enlisted men and laundresses danced to the tune of a fiddler in front of the houses on Suds Row. Susan Wallace, a laundress, was getting married to one of the master sergeants. While the washerwomen and soldiers ate and drank, Joseph sought her out. Susan claimed he tried to seduce her, with her fiancé interrupting just in time. The records include the complaint, but no official punishment aside from a private reprimand from the acting commanding officer. Joseph's diary revealed that he thought the pretty laundress was fair game because she was "so ripe and appealing." Having just proposed to Anne Egan posed no conflict for him.

•

The situation with the hidemen in Dodge City reached the flashpoint stage soon after that. A rainy spring left the roads too muddy for the hunters' big Studebaker wagons to head off into the plains in search of buffalo. Buffalo hunters were considered the dirtiest and most scabrous citizens Dodge City ever knew. The runners, who shot the animals, were not bad, but the skinners, who favored green pants and shirts, learned to live with blood and vermin from spending their days stripping the skin from the carcasses of dead buffalo. But they kept the businesses in Dodge thriving.

"Major Herriford is going to torch the town!" Tom Nixon declared to clumps of murmuring hidemen. "We can't let him do that! Dodge is our town."

Nixon swore that the soldiers were riding into Dodge. Nixon said he'd parley with the soldiers. "They've got no right to burn what's ours. Are you with us? Join us at the bridge."

Nixon spread the word and the hidemen were lined up on the town side of the bridge over the Arkansas River when Lieutenant Joseph and his troopers arrived.

The wrought iron of the bridge, recently built by army engineers, was just taking on a patina of rust. The river, swollen with snow-melt, ran below, an incongruously gentle sound. The smell of rotting buffalo hides hung over the town. The half-dozen saloons were empty and no pedestrians walked the wide main street. Dog Kelly sat at the door of his saloon with a pair of liver-and-white hounds at his feet. All the doves had retreated to their shacks or tents. The mounted troopers waited, alert. Their brass sparkled in the cold sun. The creak and jingle of the tack and the horses' snorts broke the silence.

Lieutenant Joseph studied the situation. A single bird cried from the new willows along the river. His horse danced a few steps before he reined him in.

He had expected to make a show of force by riding through the town. He hadn't expected opposition.

Nixon took a few steps onto the bridge. "There's forty buffalo guns aimed at your men," he shouted. "Take one step on this bridge and we'll fire."

After a long wait, Lieutenant Joseph gave the signal to advance. As his horse stepped forward on the bridge, Nixon fired a shot in the air. The soldiers stopped and in that silence came the icy sound of the Big Fifties being cocked. That stopped Lieutenant Joseph. He could order his men forward, but people would be killed and hurt. These weren't enemies, these weren't Indians; these were Americans. Smelly, rowdy, drunk most of the time, but not the enemy. He had to make a decision.

The men remained frozen for several long minutes, and then Lieutenant Joseph paled and said in a strained whisper, "Who are you?"

His face turned ashen and his hands shook. He looked to the right of his mount, but nobody was there.

Nixon shouted, "Don't come any further." The buffalo hunters remained poised for battle.

"My nemesis!" the lieutenant hissed.

Then a wait for a reply.

"You accuse me falsely, sir," Lieutenant Joseph said in a passionate whisper. He didn't speak loudly enough to be talking to Nixon. He drew his saber. The soldiers wondered what he was doing. They were edgy, waiting for their orders. It seemed they would be forced to fire on white Americans.

"A duel, sir," Lieutenant Joseph said in a strained voice. He seemed to listen to someone only he could hear, then he laughed. "Tomorrow at dawn, beyond the parade ground," he said, then listened to the ghostly reply. He sheathed his saber and said in a low, deadly whisper, "I'll see you in hell!"

In a moment Lieutenant Joseph came back to himself. The hidemen waited. An eerie silence stretched, then Joseph told the bugler to sound retreat. They returned to the fort without incident.

Nathaniel Joseph bathed carefully that night. Lazaro, his servant, brushed his uniform, polished the buttons and belt buckle, blacked his boots, and trimmed his hair. Joseph made the last entries in his diary. His grooming completed, he drank two ponies of bourbon and went to bed. Lazaro moved silently, tidying the rooms. Before he finished Joseph sat upright in bed and shouted, "Never!" before falling back on his pillow, still asleep.

At first light Lazaro accompanied the lieutenant to the far side of the parade ground, onto a little rise. Once up that little hill, the flat prairie stretched from the river bottomland where the fort sat, rising not more than five feet to the horizon. The inquest report said Joseph wore his full dress uniform. Joseph identified himself to the sentry, who continued his rounds. The cold dew glittered on the sere yellow grass. A meadowlark awoke and greeted the day. Joseph gave Lazaro his diary, with instructions about what to do with his kit and uniforms, his horse and his accounts, and the diary itself, which Joseph treasured. He handed Lazaro his tunic and kepi.

Lazaro later reported, "My master shout at someone, but

nobody is there." The sentry confirmed this, saying he saw only Joseph and his servant. Joseph stood silently, as though listening, then drew his saber. The disk of brazen sun emerged from the horizon. Joseph lunged and parried, his saber slashing with a silken sound. The sentry and Lazaro heard grunts and footfalls. After a few minutes, sweat beaded Joseph's forehead, but his arm never wavered. An emphatic "Ha" escaped him. He licked dry lips and coughed once, waiting for a parry.

Lazaro watched with interest. He stopped the sentry from interfering, so the man hurried back to the fort. Lazaro's role was to witness, not interfere. Once the avalanche starts, nothing can stop it. Lazaro kept his distance, kept his opaque gaze on his master. The parries and bold advances indicated the invisible enemy's moves. Lazaro expected to hear the clang of another saber.

Once, just for a second, Lazaro thought he saw the foe, the partner—another uniformed man, blue clad. A trick of the angle of the sun, perhaps.

Joseph cringed from an invisible hit on his saber arm, but his blade stayed steady. The sun's golden light poured onto the dew-damp grass, which gave off a dry broom smell. Then the final thrust caught Joseph. He gasped and pressed his free hand to his ribs. His knees crumpled and his mouth opened in an O for a last guttural moan. He fell first to one knee, then sideways, his saber still clutched in his right hand.

He lay motionless and his eyes lost their light. One leg relaxed and the saber fell from his hand.

Lazaro watched it all. He did not move or offer assistance. He did not lift or embrace his master or cushion his head with his folded rebozo. He waited, then he covered the body with Joseph's tunic and closed the eyes. He looked at the deep shadows cast by the bronze and saffron sun. After a while he turned and went to the acting commanding officer's headquarters and sat cross-legged on the porch until the officer appeared.

The post returns recorded a conversation between the commanding officer and Lazaro at the inquest later that day:

Captain Herriford: *Do you know what happened
   at the bridge?*
Lazaro: *Yes, from others.*
Herriford: *Lieutenant Joseph was talking to himself.*
Lazaro: *No, he talks to Nemesis. At night, after
   drinking. He doesn't sleep.*
Herriford: *What happened this morning?*
Lazaro: *Mi jefe intranquilidad.*
Herriford: *Uneasy?*
Lazaro: *Sí. He feared retribución, punishment.*
Herriford: *For what?*
Lazaro: *All men do things they later regret.*
Herriford: *About women?*
Lazaro: *And other affairs. A man lives his life, then
   arrepentimiento de los pecados. He must answer
   for what he does.*
Herriford: *Why didn't you stop him?*
Lazaro: *It was his destiny.*

Later that day the post surgeon examined Lieutenant Joseph's body and wrote in the post returns that Lieutenant Joseph bore no saber wound, no bullet wound, no mark of any kind.

ᑐ ✸ ᑐ

I stopped and came back to present-day Dodge City, with tourists, not buffalo hunters or troopers.

"So what do you think, Sis?" asked Dale.

"I think Joseph was Anne's lover. Then on the bridge, he saw the ghost of Captain Egan. I think they did duel, but not with any earthly weapons. I think the handsome lieutenant got his just deserts."

"But you don't know."

"No. It's a big stretch. But it *could* have happened like that."

"You take it easy," I told Dale with too much emphasis when he got up. I walked with him to the car. He walked so slowly it hurt.

☙

I made a quick tour of the rest of the museum, then found my car baking in the sun. I stopped again just outside of Dodge to look at trail ruts, but couldn't see anything and got back in my car. I knew why Dale stubbornly insisted on seeing everything in Dodge City.

I drove west from Dodge City on Highway 50. The landscape, hilly and wooded at Leavenworth, flattened to rolling green pastures at Fort Riley. Now it dried to tawny tableland. Creosote and sage appeared. Cactus and yucca grew by the road, and pastures paled to dun and amber. I knew I was several thousand feet higher, but had no sense of altitude. The flat landscape meant I could see to the horizon without trees or hills and the sky seemed higher and the sun more piercing.

A hundred miles west of Dodge City, it occurred to me that I didn't know anything about Tom, except that he tried to take care of his dad.

I had tried to capture the generous western landscape on film during my first few trips, but after a bit I left my 35mm at home. I gave up *Arizona Highways*, *New Mexico Magazine*, Sierra Club calendars, coffee table books, and Western movies.

The real landscape was always greater than anything caught in the frame. I wished my eyes and brain were bigger.

As I rolled westward I noticed the marks men made on the terrain—little towns, irrigator-soaked circles of crops. If I went through Clayton, I could see a road winding up Mount Capulin like a scar on a beautiful woman's breast. Men could harm it, but the world was beautiful.

The sky behind me gradually turned black as the afternoon passed, until I drove suspended between day and night. It was black and threatening in my rearview mirror and the sun shone ahead. I turned on the radio and listened to tornado and severe thunderstorm warnings. I wondered if I would drive out of it or if I would camp in the rain. Usually bad weather blew in from the west. I was driving west and the storm was coming from behind and it disoriented me.

CHAPTER FIVE
HASTY LAKE

~

*T*om checked into the La Junta Motel, near the turnoff to Bent's Fort. Dale rested in the reserved first-floor room while Tom unloaded the car.

After a light dinner in the motel dining room, they returned to their room. Dale cleared his throat twice, then said, "You know, I don't feel comfortable about that girl sleeping alone in a campground."

"She's perfectly safe." Tom pulled clean underwear out of his bag and hung up a clean knit shirt for tomorrow.

"You saw what the weather is like. I heard thunder."

"You worry too much. I'm sure her tent is adequate."

"What if it blows away?"

Tom heard the wind slam the first raindrops against the window. He sighed inaudibly. Might as well settle it. "What do you want me to do?"

"Go get her."

"Just like that? You know that women are insulted if you think they can't take care of themselves."

"I just have a feeling."

"She's just an acquaintance. We barely know her."

"I don't think she'd object."

"I object. How am I supposed to find her?"

"You saw the turnoff for the campground. She drives a black CRX. How many people are there going to be? I could find her." Dale rose and reached for his windbreaker.

"No, *no*," Tom grumbled. "I'll go. Sit still."

The storm built outside. It was fully dark when Tom got in the car, and raining steadily, with bursts of high wind. His headlights barely penetrated the rain. He found the sign for the campground and slowly made his way down the hill. In flashes of lightning, he saw the line of tents and campers along the lake. Men were gesticulating, then he thought he heard a gunshot, then a shot-gun blast. Maybe his dad's "feeling" was right. He scanned the campground, took a chance that she was camped alone, headed for a tent under a cottonwood, and found the CRX. When he got out of his car, he heard curses and shouts from the lakeside. He made his way carefully to the tent.

❧

Hours later, past Lamar, I had found the turnoff to John Martin Reservoir. From the top of the hill, I saw the campground stretched along one side of Hasty Lake, the result of the corps of engineers excavating for material to build the dam. It was near the site of Fort Lyons, which was now a government hospital.

Shafts of lightning chased me down the hill. The camping area was beautiful—tall, clustered trees, probably cottonwoods, a playground, and the cold blue-black water. I quickly paid for my campsite and drove to a place halfway between the lake and a rest room. All the lakeside spaces were filled, so I might as well give myself a short walk to the john. A row of tents and tepees filled in between the trees at the lake, and a half-dozen more tents were grouped nearby. Otherwise, it wasn't crowded. The sites with electrical hook-ups were all filled, but only a couple of cars parked near me.

I hurried, wondering if the rain would catch me. I got the tarp down and the shock-cords in and the rain fly over the tent. I grabbed battery lantern, food, clothes, and my tote from the car and crawled inside.

I opened my low camp chair, unzipped the windows of the tent, and watched the storm march across the high plains sky as I ate. There was no true sunset—the storm made early and artificial twilight. I was tense, waiting for the storm.

I sliced an apple and pulled grapes off the stem and cut a hunk of cheese for dinner. I never felt very hungry after driving for hours and I refused to get into the elaborate ritual of camp cooking. I would have liked a campfire, but didn't have the wood to build one. I had thought I might swim, but with the storm gathering and no hot shower if I got chilled, I passed it up.

I checked the maps and pulled a paperback by Doris Meredith out of my tote, but it was too dark and I didn't want to use my lamp. Only one family set up housekeeping nearby, in a big tent with an eating canopy. They had their own table and chairs, bicycles, and a clothesline of drying clothes.

The wind gusted from the north, stirring dust devils from the sandy soil. The temperature dropped and the sky turned a murky green. I was glad to be inside my tent and pulled a sweater out of a bag. Big cottonwoods tossed their branches. I unrolled my sleeping bag and made a trip to wash up before the last of the light faded. I was no longer just a unit of the corporation, one more terminal invisibly connected to satellites. I felt the natural rhythm of a bobbing branch or leaves running along the ground or the dance of lightning in the sky. Lake Hasty wasn't wilderness, but it was more outdoors than I usually experienced.

I treated campgrounds as outdoor motels, though. I didn't get into the camping mystique of roughing it—my air mattress and sleeping bag were comfortable. I missed my own bathroom every time I walked to the rest room. Everything got dirty, or if it rained, muddy. I was never hot for Ranger Rick. But there was something I liked about fresh air. About sleeping on the ground. About seeing more stars than the city's smog allowed. I didn't want to give that up. The price was an occasional storm. I counted the seconds between the flash of lightning and its thunder's crash. The storm was a mile away or less by full dark.

I was in my sleeping bag, but too keyed up to sleep when I heard them arrive. Cars or pickups pulled up to lakeside campsites. Two or maybe three drunken voices shouted and cursed. Who were these people? I tightened up when I heard them hollering from the lake. Drunken mountain men, buckskinners from the encampment at Bent's Fort? Locals who came to party outdoors? Ugly tourists? What were they doing here? I heard someone crash down the path to the toilets, mumbling curses. Oh, God. I had pitched my tent in the Deliverance Campground.

This was the first time I had felt uneasy in a campground in years. Car campers and RV people had a friendly courtesy, with middle-class expectations about noise and trash. This brotherhood respected the places they stayed so they were habitable for the next users. People who warned me against camping were usually noncampers, like Dale, but I didn't like the shouts and noises from the campers beside the lake.

I felt the storm grow. Cottonwoods tossed in the wind. I couldn't actually hear the lake, but I could imagine waves lapping at the weedy shore. The shouting and cursing didn't stop. The storm built. I tensed at the rush of wind in the trees and counted after the lightning flashes. The storm was getting closer.

I heard the camp attendant, a calm elderly man who lived in an RV by the gate, telling the campers by the lake to leave. They cursed him and shouted him down.

Would they leave me alone? I wondered if I could sleep even if they did. Then I heard another car drive in and more male voices, more curses, more shouts. I saw the lights go on in the attendant's RV and hoped he had a cell phone.

The wind grabbed at my tent. I had staked it, but the rain fly flapped. I heard the cottonwood branches creak. Would one fall on me?

The windows at each end of my tent were half open. I wanted to see what was happening but was afraid to stick my head up, terrified of attracting attention. I wasn't ordinarily a timid person, but now was aware of just how unprotected I was. The only weapon I had was a paring knife in my cooler.

Dale could say *I told you so*.

The tension of the storm made me nervous and the men's voices scared me. Each shriek of thunder made me jump and the electricity in the air made the hair on my neck stand up.

A car pulled up and I heard a man get out.

A fight started near the lake and I heard grunts and curses, with shouts from spectators, followed by splashing when someone went into the water. I wondered if they were all drunk, all belligerent. The storm was on us; the flash of lightning and the crack of thunder came almost simultaneously. I heard the first raindrops hit the tent.

The fight continued. The men shouted. I heard a gunshot. I was too scared to weep. The rain picked up, the patter reaching a crescendo. You weren't supposed to be under a tree in lightning. I put my sleeping bag over my head and hoped the wind wouldn't pull my tent loose and the tree wouldn't drop branches and the rain wouldn't leak through.

More cheers from the lake. It was pouring down now. Was the fight over? I heard men's shouts and footsteps moving toward the toilets. I was trapped in my tent, afraid to show myself, afraid to move. They would hear my heart hammer.

I heard footsteps approach my campsite. I froze with fear. It was full dark now with flickering light from Coleman lanterns through sheets of rain. A few pink streetlights glowed and lightning streaked over the lake. The storm was passing right over Hasty Lake.

The figure stopped by my tent. I reached for my flashlight. It wasn't much of a weapon, but it was something. A huge gust of wind made the tent jump against the pegs. The rain was even stronger now, sheeting down. Someone stood silently beside my tent. I could scarcely breathe.

The tent luffed in the vicious wind. The rain fly threatened to blow away.

Now I was more concerned about the storm and whoever stood by my tent than the men by the lake. If this was a tornado, I didn't have a chance. *Who was standing in the rain outside my tent?*

Another shriek of wind and I knew if I got out of my tent, it would blow away.

"Carla?"

"Tom, is that you?" I sounded like a little kid, my voice breathy and high. I stuck my head out of the door. "What are you doing scaring me to death?"

"Dad sent me."

"He thinks I'm some wimp—I can't take care of myself? I need rescuing?" My voice went higher and higher. I heard more gunfire—pistols and maybe a shotgun. I jumped.

"You want to stay, I'll leave you alone."

"No, no, please."

He ignored the rain that poured down, plastering his hair to his head and his windbreaker to his back.

I drew a shuddery breath and said, "Sorry. I'm glad you're here."

"I don't want to tell you what to do, but I'll help you strike your tent if you want to come to the motel. Anything breakable in the tent?"

"No, I guess."

"You're going to pull up the stakes because you know where they are and I'll pull out the shock-cords and just roll everything up and stuff it in your car. We'll worry about drying it out later."

I did as he said, then I grabbed the cooler and we collapsed the tent. Tom rolled everything up inside the wet nylon and stuffed the tent in my hatch, made sure I was locked inside the Honda, with the motor running, then he started the Vic and I followed him up the hill and out of the campground. We drove to the La Junta Motel. It was raining so hard I could scarcely see the road. I turned the heater up to high, but I couldn't stop shivering. I was wet to my underwear. I followed Tom's taillights to the neon of the motel. It didn't hit me until I got out of my car and my knees wouldn't work. I had been running on adrenalin and now it was wearing off. We hurried to the lobby.

"Your dad was right, this time," I said in a shaky voice. "I guess I better see if they have a room here."

"They do," said Tom. "You look pale."

He eased me down on a chair and gently pushed my head between my knees.

"Sorry," I said. The dizziness passed.

"Better?"

"Yes. Tell your dad I'm okay and I'll go check in."

"No hurry."

I stood up, still feeling shaky. "I think I'll live."

I walked to the desk and by the time I'd filled in the card, Dale was waiting. He opened his arms and I walked into a comforting hug.

"I knew it. I just knew it," he murmured.

I didn't say anything. I was just grateful that Dale had sent Tom and that I didn't have to spend the night scared and sleepless.

"This is the first time that's happened," I said. "But thanks."

We stood around with Dale asking questions and me answering

until Dale noticed I was shivering, then Tom and I went back outside, where the storm rumbled and rain poured steadily and there
were longer intervals between lighting flash and thunder. I got my
cooler and a bag. My room was upstairs, so Dale said good night.

Tom grabbed the floppy, dripping tent out of my trunk. He
looked stoic. How did Dale know I was in trouble? Tom tripped
on the stairs, pulled the tent into a more compact package, and
continued to my room. There was always something erotic
about a motel room. *Forget that.* But I couldn't help wondering
what Tom would do with this situation if Dale weren't along.

Once in my room I was mad all over again.

"I'm no damsel in distress, damn it. I solve my own problems."

"Hey, don't blame me. Dad had a hunch. He wouldn't give me
any peace."

"Why doesn't he think I'm competent?"

"You did leave when I got there."

I screamed. I didn't recognize the sound that came out. It hurt
my throat. It was a roar—impatient, angry, exasperated, full of
spleen.

Tom held his hands up as if to say, "Not my fault."

I was angry and it didn't make sense. He'd rescued me from a
bad night and I wanted to slug him for scaring me. I bit my lips
to keep from screaming again. He ignored my mood. He dropped
the tent on the floor, knelt, and searched for the unzipped door.
When he found it, he rummaged inside the green nylon and
pulled out my sleeping bag, lantern, flashlight, and a few other
loose items. I carried my toiletries bag into the bathroom and put
my clothes bag on a luggage rack, then sat on the bed.

"Anything else I can do?" he asked.

I tried to say "Nothing," but it didn't come out right and I
started crying. I'd done so well and hadn't gone hysterical and
now I was safe and it all caught up with me.

"Sorry." I stumbled into the bathroom for tissue.

Tom knelt and stowed the shock-cords in their bag, and draped the wet tent over the dining table by the front window.

"That's okay," I said. I had to clear my throat twice.

"I don't want to go off and leave you like this—all upset. It was a bad scene," he said. He kept his head down and didn't look at me. It was just as well. I probably looked awful. When I had prayed that I wanted to feel something, I didn't want to feel terror and resentment and anger—no, *rage*—and abject cowardice. I didn't want to feel wrenched out of my routines 'til I was shaking and shivering.

He left the tent and sat beside me on the bed. He took off his wet jacket and put his arm around me. His shirt was damp and I smelled his aftershave and sweat. His hair dried funny with tufts sticking up in back. I wanted to touch his hair, touch his face, feel his beard just beneath the skin, and feel all the warm and comforting parts of him. I put my face in his chest and cried. He put his other arm around me and said soothing things. His concern was as reassuring as his touch. Finally, I ran out of tears.

I wiped my face and blew my nose. When I looked at him, I thought I'd done something wrong. He scowled, his usual expression, and unaccountably, I wanted to make love with him, right now, both of us wet, me still shaking, water dripping off his hair. His arms were strong and it had been a long time.

I wanted to say something and I couldn't. I'd just be grateful for this moment. I was in his arms under false pretenses. He hadn't wanted to hold me. He was just being nice and I was being inappropriate.

Then he reached up and smoothed a lock of wet hair out of my eyes. That touch made me weep again. He still looked serious, but not angry. Maybe that was a tender expression. Maybe I needed for it to be. I'd take a chance.

"If your father wasn't downstairs," I began, "would you?"

"Yes, I would." He ran a rough thumb down my cheek and I couldn't breathe. "Would you want me to?"

"Yes, of course."

"We've only known each other two days."

"Right. We could be making a big mistake." I couldn't stop grinning.

"I mean, we ought to get to know each other better so that it wouldn't just be a one-night—"

"I know."

He brought his face close, and I looked in his eyes, trying to read what was there. I stretched up to kiss him. He tightened his arms. Then he pushed me away and broke the spell. I could feel his hands shake.

"Now what?" I asked.

"I'm going downstairs to sleep next to my dad."

"I'd be more fun," I teased. "And tomorrow we go to Bent's Fort and pretend this didn't happen?"

"Yes. Until I think of something. I have to stay with him. He's not well. We may have to wait 'til we get back to Kansas City. If you don't mind."

"I'll mind but I can do it." I couldn't swallow. It was the first time in a long time I'd been excited like this. Anticipation made my heart pound. This was more like it. Maybe the depression was lifting. Tom stood and I followed him to the door.

"Next time you come galloping to the rescue on your white steed," I said, "don't wait so long."

"I'll wear my red and blue leotards and flap my hero cape," he said.

I started to close the door, but he turned back, wrapped one arm around my waist, and pulled me to him for a fierce, brief kiss. "Good night," he said and walked quickly down the hall.

CHAPTER SIX
BENT'S FORT

❧

"She loved her husband so much she wondered, in her diary, if loving Sam meant she didn't love God enough." I studied the corner room at Bent's Fort. It was the only room with windows to the outside.

"You've convinced me," said Tom. He looked a little uncomfortable.

"Sorry. I get carried away about Susan Shelby Magoffin." The blocky adobe fireplace in the corner looked authentic and stylish. The fireplace ledges held a tumbler, pitcher, and candle.

"I didn't know history was so passionate."

"Well, I inferred the feelings, the emotions. I just know she loved Samuel very much. She would never have done what she did if she hadn't." The drop-leaf table had an inkwell, to acknowledge that Susan wrote in her diary when she stayed at Bent's Fort.

"Was she the first woman down the Santa Fe Trail?" Tom asked.

"Probably the first Anglo woman, certainly the first who kept a diary. She knew she was making history. I think she enjoyed every minute of it." I bent over to see if the heavy mahogany bed had rope rigging holding the mattress tick. It did. A blue and white jacquard spread covered the lumpy mattress. Knitting, yarn, and needles in a basket sat in the window.

"What happened after they left here?"

"They went to Santa Fe, of course, stayed there for a while, then went down into Mexico. She caught yellow fever in Mexico. She didn't die from it, but she didn't live to be very old." Carved wooden boxes and a washstand with a lustre pitcher completed the furnishings. When Susan stayed here, they brought her own things up from the wagon train. I would have thought there would have been more belongings scattered around the room after Susan had been there a week.

Tom and I walked back outside. We had circled the open patio on the second-floor level. Looking down, I could see visitors examine the fur press in the middle of the big patio and feel the gritty windblown dust kicked up by their feet. Last time I was at Bent's Fort I had spent a lot of money in the shop, which was run by the local historical society and carried clothes, trade beads, hats, and lots of good stuff that national park centers couldn't. I wasn't in the mood today. Besides, I was saving my money for Santa Fe, where there was a piece of silver and turquoise jewelry with my name on it. We strolled downstairs and out to the encampment.

Outside the walls, vendors had put up stalls in front of their tents where they sold drums, furs, and mountain man accoutrements. I heard the boom of black powder rifles and saw a schedule of hawk contests and tests of marksmanship. A flint knapper worked a stone and chips flew around him.

I was impressed with the apparent authenticity of the costumes and props. Men in buckskins or period clothes lounged outside tents or canvas tepees. Women in mob caps and long skirts cooked over open fires. Jewelry made of coins and bone and glass beads was displayed on tables that stood in front of some of the tents. Other tents featured racks of clothes, pottery or baskets, or reproduction black powder firearms for sale.

I read history; these people lived it. I knew they researched their period, and grew more accurate the more they learned. I could understand the appeal. In a time in America when sexuality was repressed and individuality was constrained, the mountain men symbolized license and freedom.

We found Dale sitting in a circle of women in costume. Several wore dresses with a Southwest look, the skirt and collarless camisa embroidered in bright colors, and several dressed as Indian women in buckskin dresses. An experienced beader was showing two beginners how to do the designs that decorated her high moccasins. Two women were talking about brain-cured buffalo hides.

"I'm just glad they ask me along," a silver-haired woman told Dale. She wore a drawstring blouse with a silver pin and a cap. Her stained apron had seen some action. She wore bifocal granny glasses. "I never went camping until a couple of years ago. I know they need me to help take care of the kids, but I'm glad to come. My husband, Cliff, never likes to go anyplace, so this is my chance to see a little of the country."

"You don't look old enough to have grandchildren," said Dale gallantly. She was heavyset and silver-haired, but her pink skin was smooth and unlined.

The woman ducked her head. "Aren't you nice," she murmured. "Actually, the biggest girl is my son Andy's, from an early marriage. Amy is almost fourteen and she's done this since she was little. Andy has her for the summer. And of course the little ones are Sarah's and Andy's. Sarah treats them all like they're hers."

"Is that girl Amy?" asked Dale, nodding toward a girl learning the beading.

The grandma nodded. "I never heard about divorces or custody when I was young. I guess they had it, but people didn't talk about it. Their family is working, though, so it's okay with me."

"But you come along to encampments," Dale said.

"I always loved history. My grandma came on an Orphan Train to Sabetha, Kansas, in eighteen eighty-seven."

"That must have been something," Dale said.

"Well, it gives me something to talk to Amy about. She's a good girl, even if she does wear her hair funny. I thought I'd die when she shaved part of it, but I try to remember things are different now." A small child, deliciously grubby, wearing shorts and a T-shirt, came up and threw himself on Grandma's lap. She picked him up and asked if he was hungry. He rubbed his eyes and burrowed in her bosom. She stood up to leave.

"It's been nice talking to you," she said and smiled at Dale. "I hope you have a good trip." And she walked toward the tepees pitched down by the river.

I drifted away. Tom followed and said, "I want to talk to you about tomorrow." Then Dale caught up with us.

I could hear fiddlers tuning up and we walked over to a clear area where men danced together in rustic reels. I enjoyed the rendezvous routine, but was thinking about lunch.

"This place feels like the real thing," Dale said. They stood on the sidelines and watched the men begin a dance to the wiry melodies on fiddle and mouth harp.

"I think it's the animals they keep between the walls," I said. "It smells right, anyway. Probably, with piles of furs, it smelled pretty high back then. This fort seems real, but it's the biggest fake of all."

"What's that, Sis?" Dale asked.

"William Bent tried to sell the fort to the government and they wouldn't pay him what he asked. It had been a trading post since early days and was located where the Purgatoire ran into the

Arkansas River. But they wouldn't, so in eighteen fifty-two he burned it down and blew up the walls with gunpowder. This is a reproduction from dirt up. Nothing was left, not even ruins."

"Well, they did a crackerjack job," said Dale, looking back at the building.

"Archaeologists had discovered what they could and they built it using contemporary records. So the whole thing is a fake," I said, "as fake as my interchangeable fiberglass forts. But somehow, it works. This is what it must have been like—busy, bursting with life, a place full of people."

Tom led me away, leaving Dale watching the dancers.

"Thanks for being nice to my dad."

"He's been nice to me," I responded.

"He's enjoying himself. Sometimes, when I see him talking to some woman, I think—he's had this great curiosity about them all his life. Now that he's old, he can ask questions. He goes to senior citizen things and talks to all the women, married and single. Sometimes I think he's getting foolish, but the next day he's as sharp as ever."

"I've noticed that sometimes he's accurate about every detail of a story, and then the next story will be garbled."

"So far it isn't bad and I don't want to think about the implications."

"I don't blame you."

"Well, I just wanted to say thanks." We walked back to where Dale stood, still watching the dancers. "You're so into history, how come you don't to this kind of thing?" Tom asked, indicating the costumed men and women at the encampment.

It took me a moment to answer because I had never tried to articulate it before. Why hadn't I? "These people are play-acting. The experienced ones have a persona—historical or made-up—and they pretend they are that person for the weekend. Then they go home and they're modern people. I get so absorbed that I'm afraid if I pretended to be someone else, like Susan Magoffin, I'd get so far in I might never come back. Besides, her story was so full of danger and loss, I'm not sure I could stand it."

That was the best answer I could make. I just wanted to stand near Tom and think of what we might do if we ever got together. But Tom fidgeted, then said, "You didn't tell me very much about Susan Shelby Magoffin."

"Are you being polite?"

"I like your stories. You know the history and you seem to have read between the lines more than most people."

"Historians can only say what they can document. I make inferences. I take intuitive leaps. I know how a woman feels."

"So you know Susan loved her husband very much."

"She said as much in her diary."

June 1846
My journal tells a story tonight different from what it
has ever done before. The curtain raises now with a new
scene. This is the third day since we left Brother James's.
Tuesday evening we went into Independence; there
we stayed one night only at Mr. Noland's Hotel. On
Wednesday I did some shopping.

Thursday 11th
Now the Prairie life begins! We left "the settlements"
this morning. Our mules travel well and we jogged on at
a rapid pace. The hot sun, or rather the wind which blew
pretty roughly, compelled me to seek shelter within the
carriage & a thick veil.

The teamsters were just catching up and the cracking

of whips, lowing of cattle, braying of mules, whooping
and hallowing of the men was a loud and novel scene
rather. It is disagreeable to hear so much swearing;
the animals are unruly 'tis true and worry the patience
of their drivers, but I scarcely think the men need be
so profane.

For our first supper, I ate fried ham and eggs, biscuit,
and a cup of shrub and enjoyed a good night's rest. It
was sweet indeed.

After we left Independence it took a few days to clear
wooded areas and meet the prairie with its open vistas.
My maid and I ride in the Dearborn and oh! the dust
is terrible. Samuel put us nearer the front of the train
when he saw our plight. We looked like millers with
masks of dust on our faces.

Samuel has bought trade goods—iron implements and
forged steel, also, household items such as dutch ovens
and warming pans. We have enough household goods
of our own in several wagons, plus our clothing and
personal items. We left nothing behind that we thought
would contribute to our comfort. When we stop moving
at the end of the day, I am pathetically grateful for
simple comforts a large wash basin, a chair with a
back, our own bed. Supplies to feed all the men and
animals fill several more wagons.

A few months ago I was a girl in my father's house
in Kentucky and now I am a traveling princess on a
trading expedition. If Magoffin has any doubts about the
wisdom of what he is doing, he hides them. I have been
too caught up in the excitement to be frightened, but I
shall have time now to worry as we roll westward day
after day. Will I be the woman Samuel expects? I do
want to be brave and strong and not weep or complain.

He is good to me and I find myself changing in spirit as
well as body. I pray for strength.

Saturday, 13th
We are going to "noon it" now. We are up on the
Prairie with not a tree near us. The sun is very warm.

Josiah Gregg's book prepared me for some of the
events of the trail, but he left out important things.
To me a stand of wildflowers is as important as a
mountain or rock formation. None of the flowers, of
which there are innumerable quantities and varieties,
have gone to seed as yet, so I must press them in a book
to take home. We found some beautiful roses and one
flower which, for want of a better one, I have given
the name of the "hour glass" from its peculiar shape.
It is brown and yellow, with a fuzzy pale green leaf.
The little flowers, the leaves of which turn in both
ways, up and down, are very small and hang in a
thick cluster at the top of the stem.

•

I had thought we were well underway but all sorts
of things shifted and tilted and the wagons had to be
re-packed at Westport after two days.

I cannot find one small trunk. I can only hope
it comes to light before all my available clothes
are soiled.

Last night Samuel confided that his brother James is
already en route to Santa Fe. President Polk sent him to
parley with Governor Armijo. General S. W. Kearney is
moving toward Santa Fe from the West. James's task is
to persuade Gov. Armijo to surrender to Kearney. If he
fails we may find a war instead of trade when we arrive.
Samuel is confident that James will succeed. He listens

to my timid fears, scoops them up, and devours them with his confidence.

At 110 mile creek

I can say what few women in civilized life ever could, that the first house to which my husband took me after our marriage was a tent; and my first table was a cedar one, made with only one leg and that was the tent pole.

Each day I grow more fond of Magoffin. He explained how he computes the costs against the profits on the hard goods we carry. My attention flagged and I nearly dozed when he asked my opinion about managing the teamsters. Then I came awake, as though struck by lightning. I realized he was talking to me the way Papa talks to his foreman—as though I were his business partner. We discussed the teamsters, who tend to be short-tempered amongst themselves and prone to fist-fighting. I suggested contests like foot races to work off their bad spirits. Samuel was not overly enthusiastic, but he did allow it would give them an outlet.

Samuel is kindness itself to everyone, but he paid me the supreme compliment of taking me seriously. I am 18 yrs old and have never managed anything more complicated than a Fourth of July picnic, yet he treats me as an equal although he is 20 yrs older. I'll not pine for poetry or romance when he has given me this tribute.

Last night, in his passion, I misheard what he said. "Who is she?" I demanded righteously, ready to take offense. He looked utterly nonplussed and lost his erection. (That mysterious event I have so recently learned.)

"What name?" he asked.

"You called out 'Alma, Alma.' Who is she? Some mistress you prefer to me?"

He burst into laughter. I was angry.

"*Mi alma* is Spanish," he explained. "It means 'my soul.'"

I apologized, embarrassed at my ignorance and lack of faith. He showered me with all the Spanish endearments he knew—*mi corazon, mi amor, querida.* I hope other couples arrive at pet names so affectionately. I call him *mi alma* now and no one knows our secret.

I see that I write shorter diary entries for my family than I do for myself. I must do better so that when I return they will have a record of what I observed. This is my private diary, which no one else will read.

Camp No. 7
Last night we heard a wolfish kind of serenade! Just as I had composed myself for sleep after fanning off to some other quarters the musquitoes [sic], the delightful music began. Ring, my dear, good dog was lying under my side of the bed and he flew out with a fierce bark and drove them away. Then the flying tormentors returned and it was slap! slap! while mi alma breathed sweet sleep at my side.

Diamond Spring
Last night the musquitoes were so thick I was afraid to leave the carriage and go into our tent to be closed up with them. Samuel told me to run straight into the tent and into bed without taking off hat or shoes. I dashed from the carriage through the flap and he pushed me under the musquito bar. I checked to see if I were alone, then I stripped down to my shift in an effort to cool off.

The next day I discovered that the impudent pests had left lumps the size of peas all over my face.

I sent Samuel to do the same service for Jane. Thank heavens, she is always ready for something new. For once Sandeval and Tabino got her tent up pronto and Samuel pushed her inside her net.

I am less nimble than Jane as I slowly change shape. Samuel says he can see no change, but my bodice is too snug and I must lace my stays more loosely. They are loose already because of the heat, which is oppressive. No one mentions it, so I think it must be my condition.

When Samuel returned I lay almost in a perfect stupor. The heat and stings made me perfectly sick. Samuel took off my shift and bathed me, very matter of factly. I found it unspeakably tender. Later, about 11 o'clock, mi alma came and raised me up onto my feet without waking me. He led me outside where the whole scene had entirely changed. The sky was dark, wind blew high, the atmosphere was cool and pleasant, and no musquitoes!

I thought I loved him when we married, but I did not know him well. I loved only those aspects that were public. Now I know him to be a good manager of his employees, a calm and reassuring traveling companion, and an ardent lover.

Thursday 25th
Here I am in the middle of my bed, with my feet drawn up under me like a tailor. I have taken refuge from the rain, which from the time we went to bed last night till this time, 3 P.M., has continued to fall, driving against the tent as though it would wash us away every moment. But we continue dry over head and that

is something. We rose late this morning and had nothing to do. We ate and came back to bed and sat in the middle of it to keep our feet dry. The water ran in one side of the tent and out the other like a little creek.

Mi alma soon tired of sitting with his feet as high as his head and so put his head in my lap and dozed a little and talked a little. Soon we both lay down, but not for a nap, but then Col. Owens came to see how we fared in the rain.

Whatever happens, I enjoy it still. It is one of the "varieties of life," and that is always "spice." Of course it must be enjoyed.

Each night Samuel and the wheelwright inspect all the wagons. The wooden wheels shrink inside the iron rims. The blacksmith must set up his forge and anvil and repair broken axles and shape shoes for the mules.

My duties include feeding the horses, also the chickens and ducks in their coops, and Ring, our noble brown and white hound.

We number: fourteen big wagons with six yoke of oxen each; one baggage wagon with two yoke; one dearborn carriage with two mules (which concern carries Jane and sometimes me); our carriage with two more mules; two men on mules driving loose stock consisting of nine and one half yoke of oxen, two riding horses, and three mules. Mr. Hall supervises twenty men, three of which were tent servants. Additionally, for our use: two horses, nine mules, some two hundred oxen, and the dog.

Ring is my companion during the day and sleeps beside us at night. He is hopeless for retrieving the partridges Samuel shoots. Ring knows the birds are good for something, but he has not been trained for hunting.

Besides the insect I think of as an alligator in
miniature, Jane and I are careful when we walk.
Yesterday I carelessly stepped almost onto a large
snake. It moved, and I screamed and ran off like
a ninny.

At Council Grove we found gooseberries and
raspberries and nearby, wild plums, but they were
not ripe.

Sunday, June 28th
On this my third Sunday on the Plains, my
conscience is troubled. May my heavenly father
grant me pardon for my wickedness! On this Holy
Sabbath, so much like a regular day of the week,
I took out my week's work, knitting. How could I
ever have been so unmindful of my duty and my
eternal salvation!

June 29
Cross Creek
Jane and I found enough gooseberries for a fine pie
and tonight we enjoyed a dinner of boiled chicken,
rice, and dessert of wine and gooseberry tart.

I have seen a perfect city of prairie dog dwellings,
stretching for acres. Wolves are heard at night. We
expect to see buffalo soon. A Mexican man in Col.
Owens's company died. He had consumption. Poor
man! Only yesterday I sent him soup from our camp.
Interring on the plains is necessarily very simple.
The grave is dug deep to prevent wolves from getting
to the body, then stones are put over the corpse, earth
thrown in, and sod replaced. The Mexicans always
place a cross at the grave.

July 4th

Pawnee Rock

Yesterday was a disastrous celebration. We stopped at Pawnee Rock, which has an awe-ing name since this tribe is the most treacherous and troublesome to the traders. Samuel stood by to watch if any Indian should come up on the far side of the rock while I cut my name, among the many hundreds inscribed on the rock and many of which I knew. It was not done well, for fear of Indians made me tremble and I hurried it over.

We rode briskly to overtake the wagons and had gone some six miles to Ash Creek. No water ran in the creek and the crossing looked pretty good with a tolerably steep bank. Magoffin hollered "whoa" to stop the carriage so we could get out and walk down to save the mules. But the mules kept going—over the verge. Samuel hauled on the reins. I shrieked and the carriage whirled over the edge, flew off, and crashed. The top and sides broke into pieces with a shattering noise. Samuel caught me in his arms as we fell. I was stunned at first and could not stand. Samuel carried me in his arms to a shade tree, falling once as he struggled up the bank, and rubbed my face and hands with whiskey until I came to myself. We were both bruised. He could have saved himself if he hadn't clasped me as we crashed. I should perhaps have been killed without his shoulders keeping the top off of me. I sought Jane's carriage.

I am rather the better of my bruises today. I fear I am yet to suffer for it.

We stay at Pawnee Rock. A respectable crowd now, we number seventy-five or eighty wagons of merchandise, besides those of the First Dragoons, which have joined us. I hope the soldiers' uniforms frighten any Indians that might have had plans to attack us.

We see bison now. I am uneasy when Samuel goes hunting. There is danger that the excited hunter seldom thinks of. His horse may fall and kill him; the buffalo is apt to whirl—and fatal accidents occur. To placate me, Samuel presented me with marrow and I found it a subtle and delicate dish. I have trouble keeping down the salt meat we brought. Even my father's country ham no longer tastes good. I drink shrub, mixing crushed fruit with sugar and water. It suits me better. Samuel thrives on cold food, rain, wind, accidents, and no water. I could complain, but I choose to think of this as part of our adventure together.

I can bear anything with Samuel beside me. He is strong and confident. He explained why New Mexico must become part of the United States. Manifest Destiny is a huge undertaking and we are but a small part of it. Our little train, dwarfed by the expanse of the prairie, is moving with the times.

In the early morning, I walked out a bit for exercise. I picked wildflowers until I could hold no more. Their scent faded as I plucked them and they wilted soon after, but the little spots of color in the dun and ocher grass are alluring.

All of my life I have been taught to resist temptation, to be silent, to be well-mannered, to be seen and not heard. Now I am learning I can enjoy myself and it is acceptable to Samuel. I now talk to the head teamster and give orders to the house (actually tent) servants directly. Jane washed our small clothes in the creek and they dried in an hour, where she hung them on bushes. It is getting harder to bend over. Samuel accommodates my belly now with inventive games. No matter how I feel, when I see the love in his eyes, I know I would do it all again.

Saturday 11th, Camp 31st
How gloomy the Plains have been to me today! I am sick, with sad feelings and everything around corresponds with them.

We see thousands of bison. The plain is dead level here and this morning we saw several elk, tossing their noble heads and moving with majestic pride.

Tuesday 21st
A shipwreck on land
We stopped early last afternoon with a storm blowing overhead. Spattering rain hit the carriage roof, died, and blew again. We ate supper, then the men got tents up in the loose, dry sand before the storm proper arrived. It was only eight o'clock when we went to bed, but it seemed later because of the somber sky.

The storm crashed overhead with torrents of rain, lightning shattered, and peal after peal of thunder rang. As the storm came closer, the lightning's glare and the thunder's boom were simultaneous. The ground shuddered and the tent canvas strained. My bed was a boat in a stormy sea. The rain poured down and the wind gusted. I could almost feel the tent pegs loosening.

I called to Samuel; he couldn't hear, but he must have sensed the danger because he sent Jose, Sandeval, and Tabino to remove Mrs. Magoffin, but before they could extricate me, the tent collapsed.

I screamed in horror. I struggled to brace the heavy fabric, but it weighed too much. The wet canvas

leaked where it touched me. I sobbed for Magoffin and
struggled to breathe. My big belly made me awkward
and the canvas trapped me. I felt I should drown.

Then I felt the canvas lift and Tabino hoisted it up
while the other two hauled the main pole up. Jose held
it and Sandeval pulled me out and carried me to Samuel,
who wrapped me in blankets.

"Stay here," he said and sat me inside their carriage.
"I've lashed this to the wheels of the baggage wagon to
keep it from turning over in the storm." Later, when I
calmed enough to stop shaking, I found Jane's carriage.
I couldn't sleep, but it was warmer.

The next morning Magoffin mounted a horse
bare-back with only a halter and rode through the
flooding water. He looked as charming as a mill boy
with his feet drawn almost up to the horse's back.
He drove the reluctant oxen across the racing creek.

•

Tuesday I was taken sick. We stopped at the river at
noon. We found it better to go on to the fort as two
or three companies had gone ahead and the doctor
with them.

Friday morning I was no better and mi alma sent a
man ahead to stop the doctor. Now that I am with the
doctor I am satisfied. He is a polite delicate Frenchman
from St. Louis. He is an excellent physician especially
in Female cases and I have great confidence in his
knowledge and capacity of relieving me although
mine is a complication of diseases.

•

I am terrified of being sick out here on the Plains,
even with a good nurse in Jane and the kindest husband
in the world who would gladly suffer in my stead. I am

to stay quiet in the carriage, but how can I be quiet
when every rock and rut tosses me about? I long heartily
for my mother and sisters. I am bleeding but as long as
I can feel the little one shift and move I am reassured.

How do less fortunate women face adversity? I pray
and each Sabbath read Dr. Beecher's sermons, but if I
were at home, I should give in to these discomforts and
stay in bed. Last night I gave in a little. "Mi alma,"
I said, "I feel poorly."

He took me in his arms and a groan escaped me. I am
still bruised from my crash and feel so weak. I am afraid
the child will come too soon.

"Are you ailing?" he asked tenderly.

"Yes," I said. I could not tell him all, but I think he
knew.

"I will see what I can do," he promised. He told me I
was strong and brave and that I must stay in bed and do
what the French doctor prescribed. I wish for his touch
as a child, not as a wife. I may recover yet.

July 27
Bent's Fort
On our way here I saw soldiers encamped, a novel sight
to me. The fort fills my idea of an ancient castle. It is
built of adobe, with walls very high and thick with
rounding corners. There is but one entrance. It is ninety
or a hundred feet square. Inside the fort are twenty-five
rooms, which opened on a huge patio and commons
room. Servants sprinkled the dirt floors with water
several times a day to prevent dust in the many rooms—
bed chambers, dining rooms, a blacksmith's shop, and
an ice house. Animals are kept inside the walls. They
have a well and a billiard room.

Samuel has persuaded William Bent to give us rooms and I rested in a parlor and listened to *las señoritas* of the fort while the men took our furniture up. Our room has two windows, one which looks out on the plain and the other which looked in to the patio. We take our meals in this room. Doctor Messure brought me more medicine and advises mi alma to take me to Europe. The advice is better than the medicine—anything to restore my health. I never should have consented to take the trip on the plains had it not been with the hope that it would prove beneficial, but so far my hopes have been blasted for I am rather going down hill than up and it is so bad to be sick and under a physician all the time. How prone human nature is to grumble and think one's lot harder than any one of his fellow creatures. I must quieten my rebellious heart! I am thinner by a good many pounds than when I came out.

My body has absorbed so much abuse that I feel the child is trying to escape. I feel so ill. Even with Samuel, I am dreadfully frightened.

July 30
My birthday
I felt rather strange, not surprised at its coming, this is it. I was sick! Strange sensation in my head, my back, and hips. I was obliged to lie down most of the time, and when I got up to hold my hand over my eyes.

There was the greatest possible noise in the patio.

The pains began. The doctor came, but once the waters broke, he could do nothing except attend me.

Children cried in the patio. Horses neighed, mules brayed, men scolded and fought. Servants quarreled. Nothing stopped while I labored. The pain grew and

came oftener, until I could scarcely get my breath
between spasms. I had never experienced such pain—
it grasped my body, wrung it and cast me out. And each
time I disappeared in it, another shipwreck. I screamed.
Sam disappeared, then returned, looking worried. "This
is women's work," he muttered, and left again.

"Is there nothing you can do?" I begged the doctor.
Pain stiffened me. I clawed at the bedclothes. The pain
lifted me from the bed. I thought I would split apart.
My hair lay plastered to my face and neck. If Mama
were here, she would know what to do. Mama had
lots of children. My sister would bring me a napkin
wrung out in cold water from the ice house.

I lost myself from the pain.

"Push," said the doctor. "It is time."

I had no strength left to push. I was too tired. I went
away again.

"No, madame!" The doctor raised my shoulders.
"It is almost finished. Push!"

And I reached down beyond fatigue and found
strength and pushed, felt a new, ripping pain, pushed,
and the doctor reached for the baby.

I faded and came back again. Where was the child?
I could feel all the warm wet fluids in the bed. Where
was the child?

"My baby?!"

The doctor worked at a basin of water placed on a
chest, his back to me. He shook his head.

"It was kicking this morning," I said.

He shook his head again.

"No!" I wept. I struggled to sit up. "No! Let me
see it."

I forced myself to become calm. The doctor wouldn't

do as I asked if I were hysterical. I bit my lips and tried to breathe.

"Please," I begged softly.

"It came too soon. It is too small," said the doctor. He lifted the tiny body from the water and wrapped it in a towel. He brought it to me, and helped me prop myself up to take it.

"No," I whispered. "Sometimes they are big enough."

Then I saw the tiny face, white, eyes closed, flecks of blood streaking the cheeks. The doctor hesitated, then he handed me the bundle and pushed pillows behind my head.

I unwrapped the tiny, perfect infant. I counted the fingers, all the toes. A fine swirl of black hair, long earlobes, the cord. A beautiful, perfect boy. Tears ran unabated. A fly buzzing in the room landed on the small white face. Then I knew he was dead. "No," I murmured. "Not now. I wanted you so much. You are our first child." The doctor took the bundle and covered the face.

Later, after I was again in order, Samuel went to William Bent and asked if he might bury the infant.

Outside the fort, an Indian woman, perhaps an Arapahoe, gave birth to a fine, healthy baby almost at the same time and half an hour later walked to the river and bathed.

Friday 31st July
I am forbidden to rise from my bed, but I am free to meditate. I slept, woke to weep, and slept again. Most of all I wished for my family—all the cousins and aunts and my mother, who could have told me what to expect.

I could have asked how to bear the pain. They would
have comforted me.

The Fort is agreeable enough in itself, but with it
are connected some rather unpleasant reflections—
something rather sad, though I will not murmur at
the chastening hand of Providence.

It is just twelve days since we came and eight
days since I left my room. Within that short space of
time many things have occurred, both to myself and
others . . . in a few short months I should have been a
happy mother and made the heart of a father glad, but
we were deprived of that hope.

August 4 .
On Route west of Raton
Once we left the fort, we proceeded to Santa Fe,
with me lying down in the carriage. My spirits lifted
when I gazed on the mountains. What bride lives
who had such a beginning, such despair and exaltation?
I saw rain falling miles away in a purple veil. In the
afternoon, the sun's dying rays threw claret shadows
deep into the rocks. The air was cool in the shade and
invigorating as wine. I thank God that I am mending
and anticipate further novel events. I trust Samuel,
mi alma, and pray.

Tom was silent long minutes, then he cleared his throat.

"Susan left Bent's Fort carrying her own pistol in case of an
Indian attack. She got to Santa Fe and set up housekeeping and bar-
gained with the natives selling fresh food. She must have loved Sam
very much. She had just been through the worst experience in her

life. But she never complained. She never blamed him—at least in the diary."

Tom said, "That's quite a story."

"You can see why I get into it. What could be worse?" I snuffled and blew.

We planned to rendezvous at Fort Union and I said good-bye and left.

Soon I left the plains and headed for Raton Pass.

Maybe I overreacted to Susan's story. I think I'm hardheaded and unsentimental, but Susan's story touched me. You'd think she was my best friend. Maybe she was—the colonel's lady and Judy O'Grady are sisters under the skin. Once a woman has been through a life event, she has that in common with every other woman who has been married, pregnant, raised children. The stories about army wives and Susan and other women on the frontier are universal.

The frontier was unsettled and primitive and the women needed to meet the challenges because the West meant hope, where anybody could start fresh, make a life.

The untouched landscape promised endless possibilities. They had to be worthy. They were trying to be good wives and mothers under difficult circumstances. They were the first to come to the mountains and deserts. They couldn't be weak or frightened.

They could go back east, get sick, go crazy, or die. Most of them stayed, were tempered, and grew during their time in the West.

I was glad I could just escape and that nobody expected me to show a good example. I put miles between me and home as though I could really avoid problems. I'd let the western sun burn trouble away and I'd leave regret behind—it was too heavy to get over the mountains.

CHAPTER SEVEN
FORT UNION

~

Once I got over the pass and south of Raton, I saw the grasslands meet the mountains. Maybe it was the dry air, but my perceptions seemed sharper. I thought less and sensed more. The air was thinner, drier, clearer. Sunshine was painfully bright. Wind blew without pause.

Would Tom pursue what had started in La Junta? Would I? Would he guide me up from grief's underground? Lift the lead jacket I wore?

I loved Fort Union. Nothing but grass and ruins and ghosts in the wind. The only standing walls were of the stone jail. At Fort Union I saw the prairie rise into foothills. The end of the trail was near. At the fort, the foundations and remains of walls had a purity that the restored and reconstructed forts lacked. I loved the recorded bugle calls and the living history narrations at different buildings.

Tom and Dale hadn't been here before, so they were still in the visitor center talking to the Parkie, a stout man who knew the answers to all of Dale's knowledgeable questions. Fort Union had been the quartermaster depot for the Southwest and was larger than the other forts on the Santa Fe Trail, with three thousand people working and living there.

Officers' row lined up on the south and the enlisted men's barracks on the north side of the parade ground. A flag snapped in the wind. Tiny wildflowers grew in the dry grass and scarlet paintbrush waved. In the distance, I saw a purple rainstorm move across the dark mountains.

Tom and Dale left the visitor center and walked as far as the site of the original star fort, then they returned to the visitor center. Too much for Dale? I began a clockwise circuit, studied the signs, listened to the bugle calls, looked at the storehouses. I peered into the cistern, hoping the rattlesnakes were all asleep. In less than an hour I had circled back to the visitor center. Tom joined me on the sidewalk to the hospital ruins.

"Is Dale all right?"

"He's fine. I'm glad the park person is male or Dad would wear himself out." He put his arm around my waist. I stiffened, surprised, then relaxed. He was only an inch or so taller. I slid my arm around his waist, testing it, learning his proportions. Not talk but touch was reassuring.

"You won't be able to slip into a trance at this fort," he predicted.

"Is that what I do?"

"You go somewhere inside yourself. Dad talks. You get lost."

I hadn't been aware he was noticing.

"The stories always seem alive when I'm at these places," I said. "I walk inside the buildings and I'm Alice in Historyland. The ghosts take me away."

"You like that." It was a statement.

"I guess I do. Real life is dull or sometimes like a horror movie, where you run and run and you can't escape. History is better than real life. It's all worked out. I don't wonder what will happen or where I fit in. I prefer history to real time." The women in the stories gave me courage, I thought, but didn't say it aloud.

We strolled down the path that angled off to the hospital.

"At a hospital like this a matron or hospital steward would run things, with an army doctor in charge," I said.

"I think of those Victorians as stuffy and full of grandiose honor and glory stuff." Tom brandished an imaginary saber. When he stepped off the walk the brittle grass crackled.

"That was the men. For the women it was falling in love and marrying a man and going away with him. Getting pregnant. Having babies or not being able to. Giving parties. Losing your husband. It's all pretty basic, whatever the cultural baggage or the century."

"I guess you're right," said Tom.

"Everyone who wrote about Fort Union mentioned the wind," I said. The wind was steadier here at the end of the flat plains. Cattle grazed and grass waved.

"Lizzie Simpson was the catalyst for a scandalous story—the chaplain's daughter and an enlisted man. She was young and flirtatious and probably bored with garrison life, bored with the never-ceasing wind."

～ ❁ ～

JUNE 1877

Lizzie Simpson stood with her parents just inside the parlor at the Friday hop. She noticed the young officers paying court to Katie Thornton, who was visiting her sister at Fort Union. Lizzie felt like stamping her foot and screaming, but she knew that was childish. She would look bad. Besides, she was already on probation for giggling during last Sunday's sermon and her father, the Reverend Simpson, was in a bad mood because of Colonel Dudley.

The evening was cool as summer nights are apt to be on the high grassland. Stars drew close as wind carried pine from the hills, grass from the meadows, birdcalls and animal rustlings from the canyons and valleys, spices and metal and cut wood from the depot, dust from the parade ground. Mrs. Dudley had decorated the parlor with scarlet paintbrush in crystal vases. Lizzie wanted some lemon punch, but she was used to having it fetched by a second lieutenant. The regimental band was already playing a dance tune.

Lizzie and her parents walked to the settee, where Mrs. Bess Dudley held court, with Reva Griffin, the wife of the new quartermaster, sitting beside her. There were introductions, then her parents moved away to visit with other friends. Lizzie could trail after them, looking daggers at Katie Thornton, but she decided to join Mrs. Dudley. She was curious about Mrs. Griffin, who had only arrived yesterday.

"This is a good posting, I hope you realize that," Mrs. Dudley was saying.

"It is a good promotion for Jack. After living in an adobe in Arizona, it's good to be in a regular house."

Mrs. Dudley dabbed daintily at her flushed forehead. "The problem is that Colonel Hatch is in Santa Fe. Nathan, Colonel Dudley, that is, is in charge of the fort, but the quartermaster depot, which your Jack will administer, has another commanding officer who is sixty miles away."

Lizzie wondered what that meant. Colonel Dudley had a reputation for skirmishing with other officers. Maybe Jack Griffin would be caught in the middle. Colonel Dudley could be disputatious, Lizzie's father had said. Tonight he was talking loudly and gesturing in a circle of officers when Jack Griffin left the group and walked to the settee, where he offered his wife his arm. The band struck up a polka and they danced together. Lizzie liked the way they looked at each other, almost as though they were still in love. Lizzie wanted a husband who looked at her that way.

"How are you coming with *Les Misérables*?" asked Mrs. Dudley.

"Mama helps keep me going," said Lizzie. "Sometimes the story bogs down, although of course the characters are all very interesting."

"You help your mother at home?"

"Of course. And now that Dr. Carvallo has said Papa can't go to the hospital and preach to the patients, I go every day and read Bible verses."

"I'm sure the men would rather see a pretty girl than listen to your father."

Lizzie didn't respond, but she agreed with Mrs. Dudley.

"Who is that dark man who just came in?" asked Lizzie. "With the eye patch. He looks like a pirate."

"That's Juan Romero, a trader who supplies the fort."

Jack Griffin brought Reva back to the settee and turned his attention to Colonel Dudley, who rocked in elliptical gyres, his toddy splashing over the back of his hand.

Lizzie excused herself and went to stand next to her mother's chair. Dr. Will Tipton arrived with his parents and another trader. Lizzie twisted a sky-blue grosgrain ribbon on her dress and wished she could scream. The young lieutenants were laughing and Katie was the belle of this week's hop. One held her cup of punch and another her plate of refreshments. Another offered her a small nosegay of wild flowers and two others danced around, trying to get closer. Lizzie studied her hairstyle for future reference. Katie Thornton wore a plain dress of white muslin, of a more recent cut than Lizzie had seen. She must get Mama to make her a new dress with the skirt flounced that way.

Katie didn't know yet that young women were in short supply and she didn't have to charm the young officers. They all fell in love with you anyway. Even Lieutenant French, who had said he loved Lizzie every time she let him dance with her, was buzzing around Katie tonight.

Like dogs on a bitch, she thought. She'd never be so vulgar as to say it aloud.

The Tiptons came over to greet her parents and exchange pleasantries. Lizzie had never paid much attention to their son, Will. He was older than the young officers and not around the fort much. He seemed more worldly and less susceptible to her flirting, so she wasted little charm on him. He had been back to the States to study and become a doctor. He was soft, compared to the men at the fort who were on horseback every day. He went around in a buggy treating people and he did Natural Science. Anyway, he had taken the body of that trooper who was hanged last week in Cimarron, for dissection, he said, whatever that was. It sounded horrid.

He looked nice enough. His gray suit was smart and his hair was neatly barbered. Lizzie wondered why his wife, Helene, divorced him and went back east. Then she caught his eye and smiled dimly. He offered her his hand. "May I have this dance, Miss Lizzie?"

"Certainly, Doctor Tipton," said Lizzie automatically. She made herself smile at her partner. He didn't seem very enthusiastic, either, but at least she had a partner. It was better than being utterly ignored.

Her long fair hair bobbed with the movements of the gavotte and she knew her white dress with blue ribbons became her. How could she get Will to fall in love with her? She would flirt with him and hope that Mrs. Dudley didn't notice. How tiresome it was to be always on display, always cautioned about your behavior because you were the chaplain's daughter.

She squeezed his hand a little at the end of the dance, then she managed to brush against him ever so casually, the warm softness of her cotton bosom sliding over the pearl-gray broadcloth. It got

his attention and for the next dance, a waltz, he held her a little
more closely than decorum dictated.

She was used to smiling and bantering with younger men and
she didn't know how to make conversation with this serious
man. He asked her about national politics, but she shook her
head. What could they talk about? When they stopped to catch
their breath, she asked, "What do you do when you go on your
rounds?"

"The usual—setting broken arms, lancing boils, sometimes
giving quinine or morphine."

"How fascinating." Lizzie wanted to scream. "I read and talk
to the patients in the hospital, now that Papa isn't allowed to tell
them their illnesses are punishment for sin. Dr. Carvallo complained and Colonel Dudley agreed, so Papa can't go."

Tipton snorted. Another long pause, then he asked, "How
do you find the hospital, Miss Lizzie?"

"How? Why, it's just there."

"Is it well run? Are the patients attended to?"

"I suppose so. There is a matron and orderlies and the patients
get special rations. If they're married, their wives come and help
nurse them." She had never seen another hospital. How could she
judge?

"Dr. Carvallo seems top notch, but army surgeons don't
always have the best facilities."

"I'm sure he does a good job," she murmured. She looked over
her shoulder to see what Katie Thornton was doing and the quick
turn caused her skirt to dip in front. She stepped on a petticoat,
twisted her foot, and fell sideways, nearly knocking Will down.
His hands grasped her arms above the elbows and she leaned
against him as she worked madly to disentangle her heel from the
lace on her petticoat. His grip was firm and he held her steady
until she had both feet on the floor, then he pulled her against
him briefly before he released her. At least he responded. She had

meant to make him fall in love with her, but she wouldn't choose such a clumsy way to go about it. He asked her for another dance.

"What do you suggest I do, Will? If you had to visit the hospital every day?"

"Talking to them is the kindest thing you could do. If one of them has a book, why not ask to read it? Or you could write letters for them."

"That would make the time go faster. Thank you."

Will excused himself after that set. Rather than sit with her parents, she found a chair near Mrs. Dudley. The band stopped and she heard Colonel Dudley holding forth.

"Everyone knew that teetotaling fool would come to grief sooner or later. He could do no wrong in Sheridan's eyes and that's what saved him. Courage, I'll give him courage, but no thinking. In Kansas he had more desertions than any other commanding officer. What does that tell you?"

The younger officers smiled uncomfortably. They might have held the same opinion, but there were civilians in the group and this was army gossip. Dr. Tipton listened and Lizzie could see his neck mottle red and he clenched and unclenched his soft, white hands.

"Kept a passel of relatives, lived like a lord," Dudley continued. "Goddamned taxidermist! Stuffing the animals he shot. Always needed a trophy or a medal, always played to an audience."

"Custer is a hero and a patriot!" declared Dr. Tipton. "After what happened last year, you dare to call him a fool?" Tipton's voice carried to the corners of the room.

"He was a fool, Dr. Tipton, and only his famous Custer's luck saved him. Until it ran out," said Dudley in a belligerent tone. "No tactics, no strategy. Attack, charge, that's all he knew."

"Sir!" exclaimed Dr. Tipton. The red blotches rose to his cheeks.

"Cavalry's strength is speed and mobility, sir. Attacking is usually effective." Dudley waved his glass and a splash of whiskey flew onto Tipton's lapel. "He lost more men than any Northern general. The grieving widow is trying to make him out a hero. Ha! Vainglorious fool!"

"Take that back, sir," Tipton demanded.

"Never," Dudley trumpeted.

"You are a disgrace to the army!" screamed Tipton.

"You are a shame to the human race!" Dudley's parade-ground bellow echoed in the room. "Ungodly experiments in the name of science. No gutless puppy is going to insult me in my own garrison!"

Dudley dashed the tumbler to the floor and lunged at the red-faced Tipton, who backed away. Captain Griffin grabbed one arm and a lieutenant the other. A gray-haired captain and Mr. Romero pulled Tipton away and quick-marched him out the door.

The silence stretched thick and breathless for a moment, then Dudley shook his head and walked over to sit beside his wife.

The band struck up a polka and a steward swept up the broken glass. People began talking and everyone contrived not to acknowledge what had happened. Couples moved tentatively to the floor, wondering if it were safe to come out.

Lizzie watched Jack lead Reva Griffin to the floor. They danced beautifully together. When he returned her to the settee he disappeared, probably to learn what had become of Dr. Tipton.

Lizzie sat quietly digesting what she had seen, wondering what it all meant. She was close enough to the settee to see Mrs. Griffin make a funny mistake. Lizzie would have made the same mistake. A tall man walked over to stand behind the settee. Mrs. Griffin put her hand on his and without looking began to speak.

"Do you remember when we danced all night, my dear?" Reva asked. She watched the dancing couples. "And you looked so charming in your cadet uniform, so comme il faut? That was a magic time, wasn't it, when we knew we loved each other but didn't know what that meant. I remember those dresses with hoop skirts, and the potted palms in the corners of ballrooms. I had a silver nosegay holder and my dance card dangling from my wrist and thin kid slippers that wore through in a night." She squeezed his hand.

Then Reva saw Jack enter through the front door and she pulled her hand away as she twisted around. The man in the eye patch stood in embarrassed silence.

"Oh mercy! Please forgive me. I thought you were my husband. Here he comes now. Why, you do resemble him. But you must think me a perfect ninny, going on like that."

Reva blushed and her smile looked strained. Romero shrugged.

"I assure you, madam, it was most charming. Please forgive me for not making myself known, but once you began, I didn't know how to interrupt."

"No, no. I'm embarrassed."

"Juan Diego Romero," he said and bowed. She offered him her hand properly and he kissed it. Mrs. Dudley was watching closely.

"Oh, Jack. I've just made a dreadful faux pas. I thought Señor Romero was you standing behind me and I rattled on and on. I don't think I said anything very personal."

"Nothing intimate, I assure you," said Romero. "Please, it was I who should have spoken."

When the two men stood side by side Lizzie was surprised how similar they looked—tall, dark-haired. Their coats wrinkled between the shoulder blades in the same way because they were broad shouldered. With Romero's eye patch turned away, they might have been brothers, although their features weren't similar.

Reva rose and took Jack's arm, nodded to Romero, then they walked outside. "So stupid of me," Lizzie heard Reva say.

That was the excitement for the night. After watching Katie

Thornton and fuming for a few more minutes, Lizzie told her mother she was ready to leave. When she and her parents walked down officers' row, Lizzie saw Reva and Jack Griffin standing beneath the flagpole in the center of the parade ground.

On the other side lay company quarters, quiet at this hour. Sentries marched on the hill to the north. June wind lifted Mrs. Griffin's skirts. The stars glittered overhead and the flag fluttered on its staff. Music drifted from the colonel's quarters. Lizzie saw Jack kiss Reva, who melted against him. Lizzie's heart contracted with envy.

Someday she would be a real lady, like Mrs. Griffin. She would know how to handle embarrassing situations, and how to dress elegantly and how to talk to the colonel's lady and how to be gracious.

❧

The next day after dinner, Lizzie Simpson tied the ribbon of her straw hat in a bow under her chin. She put a new steel nib and a penholder in her pocket and picked up her Bible and set off. She crossed the empty parade ground and headed for the hospital.

She did not notice the hard white sky or the wind, which flattened her skirts to her legs. Work details had left and it was too soon for afternoon stables, so there were few men around. Two red-armed laundresses bent over their tubs outside their quarters.

Lizzie did not like visiting the hospital, but it was her Christian duty. Besides, Dr. Carvallo banished Papa because he wanted all the patients to take the pledge. As an officer's daughter, she never talked to enlisted men except here. Some of them were German or Irish and talked funny. They were very polite.

The bachelor lieutenants usually paid her lots of attention, but last night at the Friday hop they fell all over themselves to talk to Katie Thornton. "Do you ride?" "Do you shoot?" They thought of nothing else. Lizzie had only danced with Dr. Tipton, who was a stick and very old—over thirty. Mama thought Lizzie should be agreeable because Tipton's family owned a huge ranch near here, but he gave her the willies and he smelled funny—like the chemicals in the hospital storeroom. Worse, Tipton had ignored her flirtatious banter and made her feel foolish. Someday she would be a great lady and he'd be sorry he hadn't treated her better.

After greeting the matron, Lizzie hurried through the first ward. The worst cases were here. One man whose mortified leg had been amputated groaned constantly as Dr. Carvallo bent over his dressing.

Convalescents lay on iron cots in the next ward. Muslin curtains filtered the light but let some air in. She spoke to some patients whose names she had learned and read Psalm 18, which asked the Lord to "show thy loving kindness" and "keep me as the apple of thy eye." She thought it was cheering. She asked if any of them wanted letters written, but they all said no.

Then, in the last room, those who were almost ready to be released lay or sat on the cots. Most were dressed. She read Psalm 18 again, then asked if any of them would like her to read to them or to have a letter written. Judah Greenlaw smiled at her.

"Would you write a note for me?" he asked.

Her heart melted when he smiled. She nodded and hurried back to the front desk for ink and paper. At least this trooper was amiable.

Once she was settled by his cot, she asked, "Who is it to?"

"My mother." He thought for a moment, then dictated:

Mrs. Hadley Greenlaw
Fox Corners
Bettendorf, Arkansas
　　Dear Mama:

He waited until Lizzie caught up.

I am in the hospital getting over a fever. Don't fret. I didn't have it bad. I know your heart grieves for what I've done, but I couldn't see anything else to do.

This occupation of soldier will keep me out of the way of Sheriff Goad a good long while. The work is hard, but I don't mind it when I am hale. I read as much as I can, but it does seem like a waste of an education. The officers' wives pass their newspapers and magazines on to us.

Say a big hello to Loyal and hug the little ones for me and take a big kiss for yourself.

Your son,

Judah

Lizzie blotted one place with her hanky and handed it to Greenlaw to sign.

"Thank you, miss." He turned out his pocket and found a penny. "For the stamp."

Lizzie took the penny. She wanted to talk to this well-spoken soldier. Usually she never noticed an enlisted man and if she did, dismissed him as mentally deficient and uncouth. If he had "wasted an education" he could write his own letters, yet he had asked her to do it.

She started to adopt the flirtatious tone of her conversation at the hops, but she stopped. It was as artificial as the painted china face of a bisque doll. For once, she wanted to be herself. Friday hop manners wouldn't work with this young man. His fine-boned face, thin from illness, was shaven. He had a long, thin nose, full lips, and a cleft in his chin.

"You don't sound like most of the enlisted men," she said. Instead of saucy glances, her eyes were down on her hands clasped in her lap. "Would you mind telling me what education you had?"

"I went through normal school while my brother Loyal tended the farm. Then I read law with an attorney in Little Rock."

"That's why you express yourself so well." Lizzie wanted to stay here and talk, watch his eyes change from green to blue with his mood. His chestnut hair was clean as laundered linen. He was pale around the eyes and the tan on his neck was going yellowish from being indoors.

"Why is the sheriff after you? What did you do?" Lizzie shook her head. "I'm such a busybody."

"Well, I guess you won't turn me in." Judah's eyes danced. "Man who had a hotel in Fort Smith took delivery of some beef cattle from the farm, then wouldn't pay me or Loyal. I got into a fight with him and got arrested. It weren't a big fight; I beat him fair, but this *thief* forged my name on the bill of sale to get back at me and said I tried to steal the steers when we took them back. My master talked to the judge, but he wouldn't have me in his office after that. I was so ashamed that I enlisted and they sent me to Jefferson Barracks, then here." He looked down at the letter. "You have excellent penmanship. Thank you again."

"I'd be pleased to come any time," Lizzie said, then realized she'd been too eager.

"I'll be released in another day or two," Judah said. "Maybe you could just stay a little longer today."

Judah's eyes were big as they looked at her and his hands pinched a fold of his trousers and flattened it, pinched and flattened.

"Which company?" she began.

"Company C, Eighth Cavalry."

And they talked for another hour, each working slowly through shyness. This soldier was nicer to her than the officers last night, showing off. He never said anything untoward, but she read longing in his eyes. After she left, she posted the letter, then went to her bedroom. She felt good about helping him. She lay on her bed and hugged her pillow. She tried to remember everything he had said and when she thought of his big eyes, her heart pounded. She had never known a hospital visit to go so fast. Judah Greenlaw was gentle and shy and she felt he knew just what she was thinking. She wondered if he thought the same thing. It made her giddy to think someone could know her true feelings. He seemed to like what he found. He wasn't like Papa, or Will, or the lieutenants, or anybody else. They all expected her to behave in certain ways. Judah Greenlaw just liked her for what she was. Tears welled up and she blotted them with her ink-stained hanky.

Two days later, she walked down Suds Row at sunset. She smelled dinners cooking and heard the sound of the enlisted men's families inside the houses. Lieutenant French came by, joked, and she had to flirt or he would think something was wrong. What she had once done easily now seemed false and forced. She tried too hard and said something about riding that had a double meaning, then pretended she didn't understand when his eyebrows went up. She continued down the row and Judah appeared as though her longing had summoned him. She wanted to shout! She longed to touch him, but she was afraid that she would make a fool of herself.

"Miss Lizzie." He looked uncomfortable.

"Private Greenlaw." Lizzie could scarcely speak. "Are you recovered?"

"Yes, ma'am. But they're giving me light duty. I'm to be schoolmaster to the officers' children."

"You'll be on post, not out on details." Mercy, she was being too eager.

"Yes, ma'am." He rubbed his hand on his leg nervously.

If a cannon had gone off, Lizzie would not have heard it. "I enjoyed our talk the other day," she whispered.

"Most ladies don't talk to soldiers. I don't want to cause trouble."

"I go to the hospital every day after dinner, about one o'clock," she said.

"If I was out walking, we might see each other."

"That would please me," she said. They stood gazing into each other's eyes in silence until a washerwoman's child bumped into Lizzie.

"It'll soon be dark," she said.

"I'd walk with you, but that wouldn't be fitting," he said. He stepped back and she nodded and stepped briskly down the walk.

A few days later, at midday, when everyone would be eating dinner, when the wind blew spatters of rain, Lizzie slipped into an empty stall in the transportation corral. It was away from the company barracks, away from officers' row. She sat in the fresh straw. She knew she was doing wrong, but she couldn't stop herself. She couldn't think at all.

Five endless minutes passed before Judah ducked in and knelt and took her hand.

"If you say no, Lizzie, I'll not touch you."

Her answer was a rain of kisses on his face. She thought she must explode. She untied her cloak. Judah took her in his arms and eased her down on it. A memory of dry grass and a man's smell and the touch of a trooper's flannel shirt against her face.

She took Judah's weight and breathed the sweet smell of him before he kissed her again. She wanted this warmth to last, but she wanted something more. She was afraid to imagine it, but she craved sweet relief. They touched. Even through her clothes, his touch excited her. His breath came in fast gulps. They kissed. And touched. She knew she shouldn't do this, but she was beyond wanting. She helped him—impatient, bursting—and they came together, then went somewhere she had never been, a place with no time, no limits. When she came back to herself, Judah smiled, his face fond and soft.

Then she noticed the rain blowing into the stall and felt the chill. Judah helped her sit up and wrapped her cloak around her.

"My love," he whispered. "Is it well with you?"

"Yes and yes."

"I have to be back in the schoolroom."

"Go on. I'll leave soon."

She picked straw off his trousers.

"I do love you, Judah."

"I love you, Lizzie." He embraced and kissed her, then slipped out of the stall.

She sat there, picking straw off her cloak, feeling warm and calm. She heard a couple of draymen enter the stables and she waited 'til they left, then walked back to officers' row.

A few nights later Lizzie waited in the empty stall again. She had slipped out of the house at midnight. A whole night with Judah—the thought made her lightheaded. She was excited and uncertain and filled with love. There was something about the dry grass smell of the hay that reminded her of when she was little, traveling on a prairie, maybe on the way to Fort Laramie, maybe when they came here to Fort Union. When she was a little girl they had rolled over the grassy swales forever. They were stopped one day for a cold lunch and the teamsters and drivers dozed in the shade of the wagons while the children played in the high grass.

The bigger children could run faster and Lizzie couldn't tag them, so she got tired of being it. She walked over the top of a little hill and looked to see if there were any buffalo in the next valley. She squatted, drew her fingers through the sand that anchored the long stems of the grass. Crouched as she was, she could no longer see anybody. She believed that if she couldn't see anyone, they couldn't see her. She sat in the prickling grass and thought about what this meant. She imagined that she could disappear in the grass, like a rabbit down a burrow, anytime she wished. Now she could stay away when her mother called and she'd never have to wash in the cold water or have the snarls pulled out of her hair. The next time her mother scolded her, she would disappear like this. Lizzie turned around and around in her hiding place, making it larger as she flattened more of the tall grass. She pulled her calico dress up to cool her legs and lay back. When she closed her eyes, the sun was a red glow behind her eyelids. She opened them and pulled a piece of grass carefully out of its clump, then chewed the moist white root. It tasted sharp and oniony and she spat it out.

"Come from Alabama," she sang, "my banjo on my knee. Goin' to Loo-siana, my true love for to see." She hummed the rest of the song. She heard a bird call and she wondered if she could catch him and put him in a cage and have him sing for her. Then she heard something rustle in the grass and she forgot the bird. Was there a snake?

I'll go back, now, Lizzie thought. It's too hot out here, anyway. So she stood and looked around. Where were the wagons? Where were the horses? She spun around in panic, looking, but all she could see was the silver-red grass. She started down the hill into the little valley, wondering where everyone had gone.

She ran. Tall grass whipped her face and arms. Grasshoppers scattered before her. Now she was crying and dust from the straw-smelling grass stuck to the tear tracks on her cheeks. She would be good. She wouldn't hide and be naughty. She'd gather the chips for the fire and never mind if there were spiders underneath. She would sit in the wagon and never say a word all day.

She stepped wrong on a rock and went face down in the grass. She rolled over, rubbed her foot, and cried. She had disappeared in the grass again. She saw only the bleached and green stems, the sandy earth, three ants hurrying. The sky burned and she heard only the whisper of the grass, smelled it dusty on her tongue. She was lost.

She never knew how long she sat there numb and hopeless, but finally she heard something, a noise different from the wind, and she stood and it was a voice calling.

"Here I am!" she cried.

Then a trooper topped the rise and started down the hill toward her.

"Here I am! Here I am!" She raised her arms and ran toward him. He spotted her. When he reached her, he swept her up in his arms. She clung to him and cried again, with relief.

The wagons were just over the last hill. So close? She buried her face in the trooper's neck where it was sunburned above his collar. His whiskers scratched her cheek. She smelled sweat and horses and coffee. His arms were so hard it was like sitting in the branches of a tree.

"Don't stray again," warned the trooper.

And now she was waiting to be found by another soldier, in the dry straw. What would become of them? How would they live? She couldn't think of the answers.

Then she heard footsteps and it was Judah and she felt his wool shirt and his arms and she said, "Here I am. Here I am."

After that they met secretly every possible chance and Lizzie knew she was pregnant when she missed her monthlies and started throwing up in the morning. She told Judah. He wanted to get married, but she knew Papa wouldn't let her marry an enlisted man. Judah wanted to go AWOL and homestead somewhere out west. Lizzie wouldn't let him. She didn't think she was strong enough to be a rancher's wife.

When she told her parents, Papa swore and shouted and Mama cried. Papa wanted a quick wedding but Lizzie wouldn't tell who it was. She had to protect Judah. She would be disgraced for going with an enlisted man and he would be dishonorably discharged. When her parents settled down, they decided to send her back to Pennsylvania to her mother's sister with a story about being a widowed bride. Indians killed her second-lieutenant husband. She would join them at their next post where nobody would know what happened.

Lizzie couldn't bear the thought of being separated from Judah. She brooded for several days while she worked out a story.

On a sun-baked afternoon in August, Lizzie went to Colonel N. A. M. Dudley. She asked his aide for privacy, then she turned to Dudley.

"Oh, Colonel Dudley, you've got to do something! Dr. Tipton made me pregnant."

The officer slapped his desk. "By God. This is scandalous! Are you certain?"

Lizzie nodded. "I visited their ranch over the Fourth of July. He took me in his carriage and did things and made me promise not to tell. It's the middle of August and I haven't. . . . Dr. Carvallo says I'm probably going to have a baby and he wouldn't do anything to help me get rid of it."

"Now, now, you mustn't do anything to harm yourself. You've told your family?"

"I can't! It would kill Papa. He couldn't live it down. Not the chaplain's daughter." What was one more lie? "You've got to do something!"

"Let me think on this," said Dudley, brushing his side whiskers.

"It can't wait very long," said Lizzie.

"Don't you worry," he said and took her hand and absently patted it.

While Lizzie looked for a trooper from Judah's company to get word to him, Colonel Dudley addressed the officers, who were drinking that afternoon in the back room at the quartermaster's. Uniformed men lounged in chairs, played cards, drank, swore, and enjoyed the late afternoon's rest before mess. Smoke from pipes hung in the slanting ruddy light.

"One of our own has been wronged. Lizzie Simpson is in the family way." A rumble of response, shifted chairs. "She has named Dr. Tipton, that scoundrel who denigrated me at one of the hops this summer."

"Sir, we must be careful. The Tiptons are civilians as well as neighbors." This from Captain Griffin, recently arrived at the post and Dudley's aide.

Dudley's chin jutted and his thick sideburns quivered. He shook his head, dismissing Griffin's words as if they were buzzing flies. "Are we going to let some namby-pamby civilian violate one of our maidens and get away with it?" He paused for dramatic effect, then thundered, fist in the air, "He must make an honest woman of Lizzie! Besides," and here Dudley's voice became low and intimate, "what did Tipton want with the corpse of that soldier who was hanged in Cimarron?"

Bored lieutenants, half drunk in the late afternoon, roused and checked their side arms. They jibed and challenged each other's bravery, never tested in battle. In less than ten minutes they were mounted. Dudley watched them with satisfaction as they assembled at the west road out of the fort. Griffin stood behind Dudley, expression bleak and noncommittal. Nothing good would come of this.

Lizzie and Judah met after dinner in their stall in the transportation corral. The drovers and teamsters had quit for the day. Mountains hid the dropping sun, but the sky was still burnished metallic blue and the constant wind blew harsh and hot.

"Is it well with you, my love?"

"Yes," said Lizzie. She had to tell him. He would want to know. How to begin? She searched his eyes. They were glassy. She brushed his hair off his forehead and found it feverish. "But you are ill." She pulled him close. His body's heat was a furnace. She pressed her palm to his forehead.

"Sometimes the fever comes back."

"Dr. Carvallo's maid from Loma Parda has typhoid and his baby took sick."

"Just the fever." He grimaced. "And a griping in the bowels."

"You must go on sick call!" Lizzie grasped his hands. Even they were burning.

"I had to see you," he said. His licked his lips. "I would sicken more if I did not."

She pressed her lips to his hot forehead. Just being near him excited her. She wanted one last time of sweet forgetfulness before she had to face the consequences of what they had done. They embraced, kneeling, and she felt his erection. He fumbled at the buttons of his tunic and she lifted her skirts. She looked up just as his eyes rolled back and he fell sideways into the hay.

Lizzie sat back and looked at Judah. His skin was yellowy-gray. His ragged breathing reminded her of a baby with croup. She couldn't leave him here, yet if she fetched somebody, they would wonder how she knew.

In the meantime, she learned later, Dudley's officers called out Dr. Tipton, who was working in his natural history laboratory, a small building in the compound at his family's ranch. Tipton denied the accusation and refused to budge. The officers threatened him with their sidearms. His mother collapsed. The officers left.

Lizzie marched to Judah's barracks. She found his sergeant and told him what had happened. His eyebrows went up, but he got two men and followed her to the corral without a word. They half carried, half dragged Judah to the hospital, but the matron said she didn't have any more beds. Typhoid was spreading through the fort, claiming soldiers and civilians alike.

The sergeant, heavier and stronger than the skinny troopers, carried Judah on his back to the barracks. They made a mournful procession. When the sergeant left the path to turn toward the barracks, Lizzie stopped him.

"Put him down." She wondered at her calm voice.

They laid him on the dusty ground. Lizzie knelt beside him and brushed his hair off his hot forehead. She heard his breathing. His eyes opened for a moment, but she didn't think he could see her. In front of the whole fort, officers' row and Suds Row, in front of barracks and corrals, under the evening's first stars, with a sliver of a moon just above the flagpole, she leaned forward and embraced him, laid her head on his chest and heard his galloping heart. Then she kissed him. She stood and the soldiers took him into his barracks.

Lizzie would have to carry on by herself.

Tom and I stared at the ruins of the hospital.

"What started out as an impulsive solution to Lizzie's problem escalated," I said. "The Tiptons complained. It led to Dudley's second court martial. During testimony Dudley turned the tables and accused the quartermaster of fraud, to get at Colonel Hatch. Typhoid spread through the fort and Dr. Carvallo's ten-month-old son died. The court martial had to be recessed."

I looked at the remains of the hospital wall.

"Then what happened?" Tom asked.

"I don't know. Lizzie disappears from the written record. Dr. Carvallo could have done an abortion, but it's not in the post returns. Maybe she died of typhoid, too."

"Or maybe she had the baby and found a husband and made a new life."

"That's a better ending."

"I was wrong," Tom said. His smile was teasing. "Even here, with only adobe ruins, you still go into a trance. Only this time you took me."

I was embarrassed. "The ghosts stole both of us." I was a

little sheepish. "As long as I don't do it in the car, and nobody gets hurt. I like the stories, and get absorbed in them, but I've never told them to anyone before so I didn't know I got lost like this."

Tom and I strolled back to the visitor center.

What was I looking for? Was this some cheap escape, some easy way to be Someone Other? I wanted to be carefree and relaxed, not lost in these sad stories. Why tell Tom a story about a woman who strayed?

We found Dale in the library discussing the star fort with the director. I joined them and asked questions about the hospital. After half an hour, conscious of the privilege we had enjoyed, we left.

Dale studied his visitor's guide to Santa Fe while he stood beside the Ford in the parking lot. We agreed to meet at Wainwright Museum the next morning. I would camp alone that night. Dale protested, but I was firm.

"I can't let one bad experience stop me," I said. "If I don't camp again, I'll always be afraid. I've stayed in this campground before and it's very nice. I do appreciate that you care whether I show up in the morning."

"After last night, I'm not happy with you camping." Dale looked stubborn.

"What can I do to convince you it's safe and I need to do it?"

Tom spoke up. "Why don't we follow you to the campsite and when we see that it's safe, we'll go on to Santa Fe."

I led the way past Las Vegas to Villanueva State Park. The road south of the interstate wound through the Pecos River valley, through villages and past vineyards to the entrance to the state park. I pulled into a campsite next to a huge camper. Tom pulled in next to me. A yappy poodle lunged at the camper's screen door and a white-haired woman with a pleasant smile scolded him. "Shush, Rollo."

Dale took in the cluster of pickups and campers at the other end of the campground, the children shrieking in the river, and a soulful teenager riding his bike on the park roads.

"Who're those fellows?" he asked, nodding toward a pair of scruffy backpackers walking through camp.

"Primitive campers. They're probably harmless."

A dark, crisp park ranger walked out of the resident's house and came down to get my fee.

"Is this park safe?" Dale demanded.

"Yes, sir," he said. "I close the gate at ten and nobody can get in without ruining their tires. You can go out, but not in." He pointed to the spikes that kept out latecomers.

"See," I said. "Perfectly safe." I was reassured by the spikes.

"I guess it's okay, Sis," Dale admitted with some reluctance.

I gave him a quick hug and stood by my car as they pulled out.

After my tent was up and I'd splashed in the river and taken a good shower, I ate, then lay on the picnic table, staring through the pine trees at the ultramarine evening sky. The red bluffs cut the wind.

What was I searching for in these stories? And if I found it, would it solve anything? Was I looking for something to explain my life or something that would make me less melancholy? What difference would it make if I did find something? I didn't have to go back to a job where I had to function. I would just keep driving and visiting museums and reading history 'til I ran out of money.

Maybe I thought I could do a Scheherazade—make up stories so fascinating that Tom would fall in love with me. Then I really would feel carefree and sexy—a lovely fantasy. I knew what it was like to be Lizzie—willful and devious. I didn't want to know the end of her story, to learn if she was punished for her sins.

I felt warm and comfortable around Tom. Maybe I was coming back to life. He didn't seem quite so suspicious around me. I was curious about making love with him. We had been together in an easy way sightseeing.

I stuck a Windham Hill tape in my Walkman and crawled into my sleeping bag. I tensed at every noise. I was awake at the end of the tape, so I got out of the tent and looked at the bright rustler's moon going down behind the bluffs across the river. Back in my tent I could see high-country stars through the mesh roof. I watched for shooting stars, thinking this was as good as sleeping. I watched the occasional satellite and airplane. I didn't want the squirrel wheel to run in my head. I finally drifted off. I awoke once and was disoriented because the moon had set. Then oblivion until I heard the familiar campground wake-up sound: the rumble as someone turned over in the bed of a pickup.

I'd camped alone again and lived through it. One thing I learned from all the good things and bad things that had happened to me in the last two years: I survived and sometimes was even better off.

CHAPTER EIGHT
SANTA FE

⁓

Santa Fe is not a real place. I knew people who lived a parallel life to the fantasy town—working, sending their children to school, avoiding the Plaza, never associating with tourism. Santa Fe was part living history, part show business. Real Indians sold jewelry under the portal at the Governor's Palace. Tourists could take as much of Santa Fe back with them as they wished.

I learned that what looked great in Santa Fe didn't look right back home. The one dress I bought several trips ago, with a gauze tiered skirt in a bright pink with fringe, looked too much like a party costume in Kansas City. I enjoyed the Santa Fe style while I was there, a visitor in a foreign country.

I always felt as though I *deserved* Santa Fe when I got there. I hadn't spent six weeks in a wagon on the trail, but it was a long drive just the same.

Santa Fe was one of the few places where the items in the shop windows stopped me dead in my tracks. Bright sun, traffic, tourists window shopping. A painting. A coat of fur and leather.

A Native American artifact. Critics derided Santa Fe's commercialism, but the town existed because people wanted to buy and sell. Once it was silver for manufactured trade goods; now it was restaurants and art for tourist dollars.

On past visits I prayed and lit candles in small adobe churches while I studied the ancient carved saints. I even got stuck in a lowrider traffic jam in Española. I cruised flea markets and resisted carved coyotes, ristras of red peppers, and crude wooden ladders to nowhere. The light was right for the saturated desert palette—warm terra cotta, bright turquoise, frost-green sage, and bleached denim.

◠

Before we left Fort Union, we had agreed to meet at the Navajo museum at the top of the city, then go through the other museums there. One price got us into five museums. We'd get some lunch on Canyon Road and continue around the plaza. I loved the top of the city. St. John's College, a Carmelite monastery, and the museums sat on the edge of paradise. I'd watched *The Milagro Beanfield War* four times just to see the mountains.

I took the Fort Union Drive exit off the interstate when I got to Santa Fe and drove to the Wheelwright Museum. I was early, but the Jacksons were already waiting. We strolled through the exhibits and I found myself telling Dale parts of my life story.

"I've got a touch of indigestion," he said after an hour or so and sat on one of the benches in the hallway. I sat with him.

"They've got great quilts in the gift shop," I reported. "My grandma Zita gave me a quilt a few years ago, a Dresden Plate made from fabric scraps from dresses she wore as a child. Grandma worked the fabric twice. The fabric in the squares was frayed and the edging was coming loose, but the pink and blue fabric had been carefully planned so that the colors started soft and pastel at one end and grew darker and more intense at the other."

"Sounds good," said Dale.

"I bought quilts at crafts fairs until I couldn't get any more into my bedroom. Now I have a quilting frame set up in front of the TV and I'm about halfway through my first quilt." I hadn't told anybody about this hobby before. "Do people always tell you everything?" I asked.

"Sometimes, if I can get them started."

"How do you do it?"

"I don't know." The old man looked into my eyes and smiled with fatherly benevolence.

"He has no agenda," said Tom. I had forgotten Tom was there. "He acts as though you are the most fascinating woman he's met and that he has all the time in the world. And he doesn't want anything."

"That's right," I said.

"Most people want something—attention, favors, approval, strokes for their ego. They want to sell you something or get something from you. Dad just likes to listen. Besides, he is the Man Who Loves Women—all women."

Dale laughed. "Why shouldn't I? They're the most beautiful, most interesting things in the world." And he meant it.

We skipped one museum because a huge show of modern art displaced the usual collection and tried the folk art museum. I enjoyed the films and the exhibits, but I was ready to quit for lunch before noon. Dale was resting more often on benches.

"Why don't you leave your car in the lot?" Tom suggested. "It's probably as safe here as anywhere. Cover up anything in the hatch."

"Thanks. It'll be nice to ride for a while."

Dale seemed grateful to quit and Tom consulted a city map so he could find Canyon Road. A box of CDs sat on the floor of the backseat—everything from good old rock and roll to Gregorian chants.

"Are you fond of Southwestern art?" I asked as we drove past boutiques and galleries.

"Me? No," said Tom. "Dad, here, has a huge collection of Indian children with chubby faces, painted on velvet."

I was afraid he *wasn't* kidding, so I said nothing, but stole a glance at Dale. Dale looked studiously noncommittal.

"I just knew you liked black velvet," I said.

"Yes, he has a bison, an eagle, and an Elvis on black velvet," said Tom.

"Young Elvis or Old Elvis?" I wondered how long I could keep this going before I said something bad.

"This is the 'Love Me Tender' Elvis," said Dale. The corners of his mouth twitched.

"That was one of my favorites," I murmured.

"I also had a Spanish señorita on black velvet," Dale said, "but I sent it to the cleaners and they ruined the paint. I was going to have it made into a bowling shirt."

"Some people have no appreciation for art." I swallowed and waited.

"I plan to buy a coyote or an eagle while I'm out here," said Dale, then he guffawed. Tom allowed a chuckle and I giggled with relief. When I thought about a black velvet bowling shirt I couldn't stop giggling.

"Serves me right for my fiberglass forts," I said.

"There's the place," Dale said and pointed at a small restaurant with a patio. He checked his tourist guide and was satisfied this was our destination.

We decided to eat on the patio since it was shaded. Vines with orange flowers grew in tubs and twined around a wrought-iron trellis. I hoped the adobe wall would keep out the smell of Canyon Road traffic.

Since Tom was driving, I ordered a Dos Equis. This was turning into a great vacation—nice people to travel with, favorite haunts, and someone attractive, if I ever took off my lead jacket. How much attraction was just that he was there? Did the gods put us together? Watching him and Dale satisfied me that they were okay.

On previous visits, I'd developed a passion for green chile salsa and now I was trying to decide if it would taste best on chicken enchiladas or chile rellenos.

Dale told us a story about a woman at the Golden Agers club who had decided he would be her next husband. He had foiled her once on the dance floor and once on a trip to Jamesport for Amish crafts, but he said, "I don't know how much longer I'll be able to keep outsmarting her. I might doze off on one of those excursions and wake up to find myself married to her. She's a nice enough woman, and she's lived an interesting life—"

"Which you got her to tell you all about," I said.

"Well, I suppose so," said Dale. "She's just a mite bossy for my taste."

I looked over at Tom. He looked almost sleepy. Today was the fourth day of our vacations, and we were just beginning to unwind. The night at Hasty Lake had delayed me. I was still waiting for that vacation languor that came when I didn't have to do anything by any particular time.

Dale started another story, then our lunches came. I hoped the green chiles weren't too hot.

After a few bites, Dale choked and coughed. When he stopped, he said, "I don't feel right." He dropped his fork and rubbed his chest and left shoulder. He looked ill, as though he might vomit.

Tom said, "Watch him," and raced to a telephone. Color drained from Dale's face. He was holding onto the edge of the table. I scooted my chair until I could lean against him and hold him steady in his chair. I could feel him lose strength.

Sweat beaded his forehead. He turned paler.

"I told you to watch out for those red chiles," I said. *Why did I have to cover up my feelings?*

He grunted, but didn't talk.

Tom returned and checked Dale's forehead. "How do you feel?"

The old man shook his head.

"Can you stand?" Tom asked. He hooked one hand under Dale's arm and helped him up. I helped from the other side. My heart was in my throat. Once on his feet Dale walked slowly out of the patio, leaning heavily on Tom. Other diners turned to look. I left bills on our table and hurried out to the car.

Tom helped Dale into the seat. Dale's color was bad and he looked frightened. I slid into the backseat without a word. Tom turned around. "You don't have to do this," he said. His blue eyes looked hooded with worry again and his mouth was a grim line. "Get a cab back to your car."

"I can't quit now. We've got three more museums to go."

∽

At St. Vincent's hospital Tom and an emergency room orderly got Dale onto a gurney. Construction made parking the big Vic confusing. I wanted to hurry, but couldn't. I was walking through lava. I didn't want to be involved in this. It wasn't my problem. But I couldn't leave.

I couldn't love Dale, after only three days. He just hooked me because he was kind and fatherly and interested and I soaked up his attention like an ignored child. Well, he was a good person and I would see this through, although my first urge was to split for Kansas City. I couldn't armor myself fast enough. Was the universe sending me disasters or was I attracting them?

The woman at the desk directed me to a waiting room, which had soothing pastel prints on the wall. A man in work clothes whispered urgently in Spanish into the pay phone. His black hair was covered with gray dust and so were his Levi's.

I pulled the lead jacket over my shoulders to muffle all sensory input. All the slick surfaces of the waiting room reflected emotions that bounced off the polished tile floors, the enameled walls, the shiny plastic chairs with their cold chrome arms. All the pathways in my brain for anxiety were deep and firm from use so that new worries jumped the synapses easily.

The lead jacket put sounds on mute. Other people's anxieties couldn't penetrate. I couldn't comprehend the terse announcements over the PA. Voices were barely audible. Vague institutional smells of ether alcohol floated on the air.

This was more familiar than it should be.

Tom came in after a long while and sat two seats down. His face told a bleak story. "They're trying to stabilize him so they can move him to a room."

"A heart attack?"

"Yes."

"This has happened before." It was a statement and I knew it was right.

"Yes."

"So this is why you looked worried before."

"Partly. He insisted he wanted a trip. He didn't say 'one last trip,' but I knew that was what he meant. I was afraid everything would be for the last time and if we didn't come, we'd never do it."

"I know."

Tom looked at me funny. Then he said, "It's nice of you to hang around, but this isn't your problem."

"I feel I'm a part of this. I guess I should have told you—my dad died last winter, February." I remembered the cutting wind on the hill at Mount Olivet, the brilliant winter sun, tears running icy trails on my cheeks. I got cold and couldn't warm up.

"That explains why you were so jumpy."

"I didn't know it showed."

Tom looked up every time a hospital employee moved. I didn't know what I could do for either of them. I remembered when my dad was sick; I always had somebody's shoulder to cry on when I needed it. The aunts, those harpies who would criticize your lipstick if they couldn't find anything else, were rocks of strength. They kept my mother going and propped up my sisters and me and fed everybody until we started coming back to life.

Tom probably didn't cry, but maybe he would appreciate somebody who wouldn't freak out if he did get upset.

"Do you mind if I stay?" I asked.

"Of course not," Tom replied.

"I don't want to intrude, but sometimes it's good to have somebody around."

"Please don't go." Tom's voice went thin and he clamped his mouth shut and closed his eyes. He took deep ragged breaths. After a few minutes he grew calmer. I wanted to hold his hand, but didn't.

"I hate to sound like a wimp," he said. "My mother died. My daughter lives out of state with her mother. That's almost like losing her. It was my own fault and I could have done something. Now, I'm helpless and it hits me hard. He's all I have."

"Tell me about your daughter," I said.

"I told you I had a band, The Englewoods." Tom looked away, remembering. "We went to high school together. We started playing for school dances, when they'd let us. I was lead guitar and Sean had the best voice and Joe played bass. Julie and I started dating before we graduated from Van Horn. I thought she was the smartest, most beautiful girl in the world and I never wanted to lose her. I remember the night. We were parked on the road beside Mount Washington Cemetery. The windows started to steam up. 'Would you marry me?' I asked and she said yes. She got a job and so did I. She took college classes at night. I practiced with The Englewoods and the group started getting gigs around town."

"Would I have heard you?" I asked.

"If you went to places around Kansas City in eighty-five or eighty-six, along about then."

"I was too young. But the name sounds familiar."

"We had a little success. We got some out-of-town bookings. We thought we were on our way."

Tom got up and walked back and forth in front of the row of waiting room seats. He ran his hands through his hair. He walked up to the double doors and looked in, then came back.

"I had a chance to grow up with Mattie, my little girl, and I blew it. I didn't know that's what I was doing. I just couldn't give up the music."

"How old were you?"

"Nineteen."

"That's not very old. We all make mistakes."

"Well, Julie divorced me. She got promoted at the insurance company, took Mattie, and moved to California, Orange County."

"Do you see her?"

"Every year for a month. She comes to Kansas City. She said she doesn't want to come next year; she's got some summer program she wants to do. She's really smart. It's computer camp."

"So you're losing her, too." I wished I wouldn't blurt out things like that. Tom squeezed his eyes shut again.

After that, neither of us could keep the conversation going. At last a very young doctor walked up to Tom.

"He's resting now. We're going to admit him and keep him a couple of days. I need a history from you."

"How is he?"

"If this was the first or he were younger, I'd say his chances were fine. But I understand this is not the first."

"No," said Tom. And he pulled out his billfold and removed a folded sheet of paper. It listed years and dates of hospital visits, prognoses, and meds. The doctor sat down and copied the information onto a form on his clipboard.

"I should have warned you," Tom said to me.

I said nothing.

"At first it didn't seem important, then—"

I waited.

"I was afraid you'd take off."

"I might have at first," I admitted, "but I'm here now." It felt good—hearing that he wanted me to stay.

"I didn't mean for it to be a secret. This is not much of a holiday for you."

"I'm okay with it." And I looked at the sheet and learned Dale had been going downhill for a couple of years.

"And you let him talk you into this trip." I knew how much I had wanted this trip and I didn't have Dale's sense of time running out.

"He said he was tired of traveling on a bus with 'those old folks' and I wanted to spend some time with him." Tom shook his head and ran his hands through his hair.

"It's hard to say no." I was exercising my talent for stating the obvious.

Tom nodded and hung his head. I wanted to take him in my arms and say, "It's okay to cry. I understand." I took his hand instead, for a minute. I noted the thick calluses, a few dried cuts, and the warmth.

Eventually, a nurse told us we could go upstairs and we followed Dale's gurney. An IV dripped into his arm. I waited on the floor until I was allowed in his room. An EKG readout traveled across a monitor above his bed.

For a bad moment I was back in the room at St. Luke's in Kansas City, my father's gray hair brushed back from his pale face. He lay sleeping while a football game played silently on the TV. I watched, but nothing registered. Whenever I saw football on TV, with green, green grass and intent players, I remembered my father dying.

Dale looked gray, exhausted, and very ill. He opened his eyes, tried to smile, then drifted off again. Tom went looking for the doctor. I held Dale's hand—the one without the IV. It was too cool. He breathed steadily. The readout ran smoothly. Maybe he would be okay after all.

I looked out the window at the traffic on St. Michael's Drive and realized it was rush hour and we'd never finished lunch. As if to confirm, my stomach growled.

Tom came back and said, "They're taking good care of him. They've talked to his doctor in Kansas City. They'll watch him a couple of days, do tests, then I can take him home."

"In an ambulance?"

"I don't know. I didn't think to ask. My brain isn't working right."

I remembered what it was like. "I need some dinner. How about you?"

He looked nonplussed. "Yeah, now that I think of it."

"There's sure to be a cafeteria somewhere, or a coffee shop."

"Right. Sure."

Dulled emotion bounced off the slick floors and handrails and window glass. Noise from the cafeteria penetrated the urgent hush of the halls. Trays clattered, dishes and silver rattled, the swinging doors to the kitchen thumped. The steam table's smell was universal—overcooked vegetables, subdued meat, and starchy stuff to fill in.

Then a satisfying whiff of onions and beef reached me. My stomach growled. Suddenly I was very hungry. I took a little casserole of beef stew and every vegetable and a dinner roll. Tom took fried chicken, the stew, and mashed potatoes. The dinner crowd hadn't arrived and a few groups and singles sat at tables evenly spaced through the room.

The food restored us. I felt my blood sugar rise. Tom looked blasted. Love is a harsh and dreadful thing, said the Grand Inquisitor.

If I never loved anybody, I'd never feel pain. I wouldn't need the lead jacket. Watching Tom hurt was hard, too. I noticed he had become softer and more accessible. He was younger. His caring made him approachable.

Desire fought its way out of the lead jacket. I'd spent three days with him and nothing he did or said hit me the wrong way. I hadn't had to throw up barriers against him. I felt my shoulders relax. The beef stew's browned crust collapsed under my fork. The chewy beef was tender, glazed with herb-flecked gravy. Chiles made it spicy. I couldn't say when I'd eaten better stew.

The late afternoon sun threw shadows into the terra cotta town that climbed the hills outside the windows.

A piece of Tom's hair stuck up funny in back. He'd missed a gob of gravy on his chin. He forked more mashed potatoes into his mouth. We'd avoided sex but our concern linked us. We had our Ship of Fools fellowship and storyteller/audience relationship and our looking-out-for-Dale common ground. Now this.

I couldn't say anything, but I looked at him and felt my face stretch into a smile I couldn't stop. I wanted to reach him before he regained control and firmed up, before his patient, standoffish mask went back in place. I wished for some guaranteed icebreaker, some flirty come-on thing to say, but I was blank. I just smiled. I reached over and took his free hand and squeezed it. He looked up at me and returned the smile. He turned his hand so he could squeeze back. I felt warm and full and happy.

"Do you plan to stay at the hospital tonight?" I asked.

"No point," he said. "I can't do anything. Besides, I get buggy in hospitals. I'm going back to the motel."

"If you really want a break tomorrow, I know some interesting places in Santa Fe. You wouldn't be far away."

"You don't have to plan your holiday around this."

"I do these things anyway. Besides, you'll need a break."

"We'll see how he is tomorrow."

CHAPTER NINE
CHIMAYÓ

~

*T*he next morning it took me a long time to get to Santa Fe. I had fallen asleep as soon as I got in my tent. In the morning I felt hungover and everything seemed to take a long time. Anxiety slowed me. It took an hour—swimming in the river, eating the last apple from my cooler—before I could decide to take down my tent. It would be easier to stay in a motel in Santa Fe and visit the hospital without an hour's drive. It took roughly forever to strike the tent, fold it, and stow all my gear in the CRX. Eventually I showered, dressed, and got to the hospital.

Tom sat beside Dale's bed. The old man was awake and whispered, "Morning, Sis."

I bent and kissed his forehead. "Are you behaving yourself?"

Dale smiled.

Then I looked at Tom and he smiled a little, too. Later, in the hall I asked, "How is he really?"

"A little better. The doctor was guardedly optimistic."

"You know him. What do you think?"

"I can't tell. I'm still scared to death he'll pop off. He doesn't look good." Tom stopped. "He doesn't give up, though. The doctor is coming again this morning and I'm waiting for him. Then lunch. I need to get out of here for a while."

I went back in and sat beside the bed, and took Dale's hand. He smiled. "If this is the end of the trail, at least I got here." I started to protest, but he shook his head. "I feel loads better, ready to hit another museum, or go on with Tom. But if this is it, it's been a good run."

I couldn't say anything. I held his hand until he fell asleep. Then I stared out the window at the piñon-and-adobe town. How do you stare down death? Do you skitter away, hope to escape? Or just set your teeth and prepare for the worst? I didn't want to think of the worst.

The young doctor eventually arrived and looked at Dale and checked his chart. Then he and Tom left together. I wanted to be in on the conference, but knew I had no right.

When he came back in the hospital room, Tom said, "Let's get out of here."

"Any change?" I asked.

"Not really." Tom strode down the hall, then he realized I was running to keep up and slowed his pace.

"Why don't I drive?" I suggested.

"Okay. You choose."

I stopped and phoned Jaramillo's Restaurant and made a reservation. As long as I kept moving, I was safe. Being alone in the car with Tom excited me. I was afraid I was a love junkie, ready to get high on each new man. I told myself Tom couldn't read my mind. I calmed down to a state of being pleasantly interested.

Driving down the highway to Chimayó, I saw signs for the turnoff for Los Alamos. One trip to New Mexico I drove to Los Alamos. I knew some of the wartime history, had read the novel *Stallion Gate*, and seen documentaries. All the Manhattan

Project drama paled at the museum, a repository of scientific information. I moved from one display to the next, trying to understand the technical stuff, and after a while it dawned that Los Alamos was a place devoted to killing people. I left with a bad taste in my mouth and drove straight to the chapel at Chimayó, where I sat amid the *santos* until the feeling passed.

Los Alamos had to be in New Mexico. But not because Oppenheimer had been to prep school here or because the mesa provided good security. Only here could the profound, abiding Native and Hispanic spirituality counteract the evil of that place that made death.

Today Tom and I drove the winding road to Chimayó, once a separate village north of Santa Fe, but now connected to the city by shops and subdivisions. I sort of remembered where the church was and sort of followed the signs. It felt as though we would never get there and that it was too far from the hospital, but it had only been half an hour. I went in one of the shops selling religious items and bought a tall votive candle.

Tom's eyebrows went up.

I shrugged. "It can't hurt. Besides, that's what's wrong with Jerry Falwell—those Protestants don't do candles or incense. No Gregorian chants. No penitential rites. No *santos* or *retablos*, none of that good stuff."

"If you say so."

I bought a *milagro*, a brass charm, in the shape of a heart. I could choose legs, arms, heads, or entire bodies from the display case, but decided the heart was enough. I safety-pinned the brass charm to my shirt. I'd leave it in the chapel with prayers for Dale's heart.

I didn't know what it was about Chimayó—true, it was a beautiful example of northern New Mexico church architecture, very old, very well maintained. But I felt something darker and more powerful.

We walked through the arched entry to the churchyard. Tom picked up a brochure on our way into the church. I genuflected automatically and slid into a pew and Tom sat beside me, reading. I said the usual prayers, then got up and searched the stand until I found a place for my candle. I lit it, then returned to the pew. I could identify most of the images of the saints by the items they carried. Here Jesus wore moccasins and El Santo Niño de Atocha wore out tiny running shoes doing good deeds. I always looked for San Rafael carrying a fish. I never saw a San Rafael in Kansas City. Saint James, Santiago, on a horse stood near the altar.

The church was seventeenth century, and some of the *bultos* were equally old. I always like the folk-art atmosphere in New Mexico churches. Adobe has to be replastered often to keep from deteriorating. The wooden floors had splintered from thousands of scrubbings. The smoke from candles had darkened the walls and ceiling. It looked almost too perfect, but a posted mass schedule told me it was still a church and not just a tourist destination.

Old churches were often built over pagan temples and I wondered whose bones lay beneath the rough floor here. People came for miracles. For centuries pilgrims had walked hundreds of miles to pray.

Tom and I ducked through a low door to a room adjoining the chapel. It was fifteen degrees warmer there from all the candles burning. The walls were covered with framed testimonies of healing, handwritten letters, newspaper clippings, and snapshots. Braces and crutches littered the corners. Images of the Virgin and El Niño were replicated throughout the room. I gave Tom a moment to take it all in. It was primitive and vulgar and, for me, profoundly moving. People had come hoping for something and got it and returned to give thanks and leave a record. I went into the back room where two women in jeans and sweatshirts, one holding a baby, knelt in prayer, and an elegantly dressed woman scraped dirt out of a hole in the floor into a black plastic film can.

"So that's the miraculous dirt," Tom said.

"Yes," I said. I fished an empty plastic pill vial out of my purse and bent. When the woman was finished, I scraped dirt from the bottom and sides of the foot-wide hole into my bottle, capped it, and put it in my pocket. I licked a smudge of dirt off my middle finger. Tom watched. People had been digging up miracle dirt here for hundreds of years, but the hole never got deeper.

I left my milagro at the feet of one of the Virgins of Guadalupe. Once I let it go, pain and longing and hope poured out in a disjointed prayer. I wanted to keep that old man in my life. Nobody listened better, nobody loved women better. *Don't take Dale.* If miracles could happen, it would be from here, from people kneeling on elemental earth. Maybe they all had doubts. Maybe they all said, this may be nonsense, but I'm willing to be a fool to help someone.

"I think we should eat and get back," Tom said when I came out, so we went directly to Jaramillo's, bypassing weaving shops and souvenir stands where ristras of fresh, drying red peppers hung.

The restaurant had expanded onto a patio outside the back door, then, as business increased, two additional levels were cut into the steep hill behind the building. When the maitre d' asked, I said yes and he led us up to the middle level, where we were partially shaded by a small tree.

"This is nice," Tom said. I nodded. To the east, the air filled with rose, rust, pink color from the Sangre de Cristo Mountains. Cirrus clouds broke the steady blue of the sky. We saw the next range west in the distance. The clouds chased the sun, giving moments of shade.

Tom looked distracted. Nothing outward gave him away—his shirt was impeccable, his jeans pressed, his hair combed. But he seemed mentally disheveled. I had taken him out of the hospital, but not away from the worries. I had dressed as carefully as I could that morning, but my clothes were wrinkled from being packed and it's hard to put makeup on in a campground shower room. We looked like a nice couple, enjoying a holiday. Appearances deceive.

After we ordered, Tom asked, "Do you believe in that? Back at the chapel?"

"You sound like you don't."

"Sorry, I'm too rational or too Protestant or too Anglo to get into it."

"I figure for Dale, I'll do what I can."

"I don't mean to be disrespectful—"

Which I took to mean that he thought I was an idiot.

"—but miracle dirt can't do anything for my father. He needs an EKG and tests and blood thinners."

I felt myself becoming defensive. The dirt had no magic chemical or bacteria. "They're finding every day that a person's attitude has a lot to do with his health."

"This is medieval." Tom stared at his Coca-Cola.

I felt myself sweating. Standing up for what I believed always took more effort than I wanted to admit, but if I didn't, I'd be sorry afterward. I gripped my coffee cup more tightly. I thought about the room next to the chapel. "You sound like an agnostic anthropologist describing some primitive religious practice."

"Maybe I am. It's superstition to me," Tom replied. "In another age, people were simpler. Or their religion was simpler. It's too easy. Dig up some dirt and say a prayer."

"There are more things in heaven and earth, Horatio, than are dreamt of in your philosophy. More happens in the world than I can explain with logic and science. Chimayó dirt reminds me that I don't run the universe, that there's something I can't control out there."

"I can't argue with faith." His tone of voice said he didn't believe a word, but was too polite to continue the discussion.

Thick tension separated us. Neither could see the other

clearly, neither could quite hear what the other was saying. Tom looked beyond the patio, at the foothills with houses and trees.

"Anthropologists sound patronizing and superior," I said. "But really, they can be rational because they don't know. It's like someone who's never been in love saying it doesn't happen. They aren't superior; they just don't get it."

"I get it!" Tom sounded exasperated. "I just don't get this particular thing."

"What kind of religious experience have you had?" I tried to sound neutral, but I heard some sarcasm bleed through. I wanted to change the subject.

"Not religion. Music."

"So you had music experiences."

"It's hard to explain." Tom looked uncomfortable. He probably wasn't used to talking about this kind of thing.

"Religious experiences are indescribable—that's supposed to be one of their characteristics." I sipped my coffee.

Tom thought a moment, then said, "I find my way to a different state of mind through music, *making* music. I get out of myself. Even with the other guys playing. When it all goes right, I'm part of something bigger than just my single self. Sometimes from just listening."

"That sounds wonderful," I said. "Do you make music now?"

"I quit, actually." His voice changed, but I didn't know what that meant. When my voice changed like that, it usually meant I was hiding emotions.

"So when you were young, you were a musician. I bet you had hair down your back, and frayed jeans, and tie-dyed T-shirts."

Tom allowed a small smile. "Yes, and decals all over my guitar case."

"It sounds like a lot more fun than just going to school, which is what I did. What was it like?"

"What was it like?"

"We started fooling around with our guitars, then after a while we started getting gigs. I was a big promoter, never took no for an answer. Finally, we were playing every weekend, sometimes in Lawrence and Columbia. A couple of times in Emporia and Pittsburg—college towns. Dale didn't like it."

"I remember one day most clearly. He and I are in the garage. The hood of the Mustang is up. There's gray primer and body putty. Wires from the amplifiers for the guitars snake along the floor. It's a little cold and I've been doing chords. He's just home from work. It smells a little like old burned motor oil and gasoline. Sun is coming through the dirty windows."

"You can't keep on like this, Son," Dale said.

Tom braced himself for another lecture. He tossed his head so his hair masked his eyes. Dale said, "You should be working and taking care of Julie."

"We're going to break through any day now," Tom said. "I called that agent who gave us his card last week." He turned and picked up a guitar, plucked the strings.

"You quit going to classes again," Dale said. He sounded more sad than accusing. He looked around the garage. The overhead light revealed a torn-down alternator sitting on the tool bench.

"Well, you don't have to go to college to make music. It's all I want to do." Tom kept his head down, avoiding Dale's eye.

"You shouldn't have married Julie right out of high school if you didn't want to be married to her."

"I never wanted to be married to anybody else." Two loud chords. "She understands."

"She's having a baby and you aren't working."

"She's working and she's got good insurance. It'll be okay."

Tom looked at Dale in his work clothes—solid, eternal—with his crew cut and his safety shoes, still neat after a day's work.

Dale looked weary. "I'm tired of talking to you. I only want you to be happy. And I don't think this will make you happy in the long run. When you make promises you don't keep—like taking care of Julie—you lose your self-respect. I don't think music gives it back. You can't expect me and Julie to support you the rest of your life. As long as you can practice here and let her pay the bills, you'll never grow up. You can't live like a teenager forever. Growing up ain't so bad. You have a good relationship with your wife, you pay your bills—it's satisfying, in the long run."

Dale couldn't understand, so Tom didn't even try to explain. People had always responded to his music. He could make excitement. He could make them understand if they would listen. But Dale just couldn't hear the music the way he heard it. Tom wanted to get inside the music. That was where he really lived.

Later that night the other members of his band showed up. Sean argued with them until they got the accompaniment just right for the song he had written. It wasn't a great song, but Sean liked it and sang it as well as it could be sung.

They raided the fridge about ten and Tom phoned Julie to tell her he would be late, then they were back on the cold cement, with the amps vibrating, the wires snaking across the room. Joe's steady bass, Sean on keyboard, him on lead guitar. The great sound they could make together, the shock to learn it was after midnight when they quit.

❧ ✿ ❧

"I can still see him that day in the garage. I still cringe at the kid who thought his dad was square and too dumb to understand. There was something about those work clothes—tan polyester.

That crease in the pants. That sheen old clothes get. His belly straining the buttons on the long-sleeve shirt. His belt with the finish almost worn off. And his short hair. Nobody with short hair said anything I wanted to hear. I still don't do everything he says, but I listen. He knew what was really important."

When we finished eating, I wanted to dawdle. It was pleasant in the shade, with a little breeze. I didn't want to go back to St. Vincent's Hospital. I wanted to wait there until the mountains turned carnelian, rose, blood-red when the day hurried toward its end.

"So now you just listen, you don't make music?"

"Yes."

"You're not going to tell me any more?"

Tom took a deep breath. "Well, I might as well. You probably think I'm some Nice Son Who Takes Care of His Father. I kinda like that—makes me feel good. But when Julie told me she was pregnant, I still didn't get a job. Finally, she took Mattie and left." He looked away, not at me but at the woman who left.

"I got the divorce papers in the mail. I should have contested the visitation, but everything was coming apart. I was twenty-one. I had about three semesters of college credit, no job history, an ex-wife and child, with support to pay. I quit. It was too late to keep Julie; I'd lost Mattie. But the lawyer made it very plain: child support. Something happened after she left. I lost heart for music. Went to DeVry, took enough computer classes to get a job. I switched to UMKC. It took six years going part-time to finish my degree. I'm good at what I do—writing programs. Sometimes it seems like a huge computer game to make it all work, find the groove. Then people want it yesterday and my director gets on my back and it feels like work."

"It sounds as though you punished yourself, quitting music."

"Oh, I still fool around a little. But what was the point? I was trying for some impossible high while the really good parts of life got away."

"Surely, you've had girlfriends since." I hoped he had.

"Right, girlfriends. I was even engaged once. I've known some fine women. I didn't think it would be hard to find somebody. It was so easy when I was a kid. Julie was just there and it happened. I let Julie get away, then I found out it wasn't easy. I haven't found anybody else who felt like she did, acted like she did. Every time I get close to a woman, I try too hard and they get away. The last time, well, it didn't work out." He sounded bitter.

"I know how that feels," I replied.

"Mattie and I have a good time when she comes. I taught her enough guitar chords to play most of the songs she wants to play. We travel, we camp, we went to Washington, D.C., last month. It's not like having her in my life, but we get along pretty well." Tom looked at the sky again. "Dad was glad I started acting responsible."

"How old is Mattie?"

"Fourteen. Quite a young lady. I don't like the tattoo, but at least she let her hair grow out."

He was quiet on the drive back. Now I had a hint why he was angry, why he was suspicious.

෴

When we got back to Santa Fe I asked if he wanted to stop at his motel (no) or a bookstore (yes). He bought a Clive Cussler thriller, then I dropped him off at the hospital about four and drove back to Cerrillos Road. The second motel had a room, a miracle during tourist season. I was in the funky older part of Santa Fe. I don't spend much time in a motel room when I'm on vacation, so I didn't see any point in paying very much, as long as it was clean.

Tom and Dale were talking when I entered the hospital room later. Dale was propped up and seemed a little brighter.

"Did you bring me any supper, Sis?" he asked. "They don't give me anything but Jell-O. I want carne adovada—only part of the country where you can get it."

"I'll get some carry-out next time," I promised.

How could I get some of the Chimayó dirt to Dale? I couldn't expect a sick old man to consume dirt, of all things. And the nurses would kill me.

Tom looked slightly less worried now that his father was improving. I was relieved. Dale soon tired and drifted off to sleep. When Tom left for a moment, I took a grain of Chimayó dirt and rubbed it on Dale's hand and kissed it. I prayed the standard prayers, then added my own intense hopes. Tom and I stayed 'til the end of visiting hours.

We rendezvoused at a bar in a mall for a beer.

"I feel like I should say something." Tom pulled on a longneck Budweiser. "We almost started something at Bent's Fort."

"Dale is on your mind," I said. I printed damp circles on the tabletop with the bottom of the beer bottle. And something else keeps you angry, I thought.

"You've hardly made any jokes all day," Tom observed.

"Joking is how I cope."

"It's your defense."

"I had some bad times. Cracking dumb jokes and smarting off is one way to get through it."

"What kind of bad times?" Tom asked.

This was no time for a confession. "Maybe we'll get around to that some time," I said. "You told me a little about yourself—"

"I felt I owed you some history after what's happened."

We drank and sat without talking for a while. A new Garth Brooks song came on the jukebox.

"Did you give Dad some of that dirt?" he asked.

"Would I tell you if I had?"

Tom laughed a little, an end-of-the-day release. He paused. "If Dad weren't sick. If we went to Canyon de Chelly and had more time together. If we had some time alone with nothing on our minds—"

"We might get to be friends," I finished.

"Maybe more than that," he said.

"You could have fooled me. You've been a perfect gentleman. No agenda except Dale."

"Well, I've been burned. Women turn to smoke in my hands. The last time, well, when I found out she was sleeping with Bruce—" Tom's jaw tightened and I wondered what he was biting back. "Bruce and I've gone fishing together with a bunch of guys every spring and fall for years. He introduced me to Roxie. They work together at an accounting firm on the Plaza. He was already going with another girl. Roxie was tiny, dark hair, Cajun from New Orleans. She was perfect—little body, sweet face, hair." Tom took a hit of his beer.

"We went together for six months or so and we were talking about getting married. Then I find out Bruce and Roxie were sleeping together. It just tore me up. My best friend and my girl! I wished I could take an Uzi to the office where they worked and spray everybody there. I particularly wanted to kill both of them."

"If they'd told me, I guess I'd have to take it. But they were doing it and Roxie was still going out with me and we were talking about getting married. I thought about how I would go to her apartment and wait 'til she came home and beg her to stop. Or take my imaginary Uzi and let her have it. I didn't know what to do, so I just stopped everything. Except I couldn't stop thinking about her, but I didn't phone, didn't try to see her. I couldn't face what I'd found out."

He fell silent and I didn't know what to say. Now I knew what kept him angry under his mask.

"You still carrying a torch?"

"I suppose. It's been long enough, but I haven't gotten serious about anybody else. It feels like a dream—I'm walking along, trying to do the right thing this time and I reach for her—and she turns to dust in my hand."

"But you think I won't?"

"I'd like a chance to find out." He smiled—a funny, sad smile, as though he wasn't sure.

"That Custer story must have hit close to home," I said. "I didn't know anything about you and Roxie. We'd just met, and it really did happen to the Custers."

"I wondered if you were telling it to bug me."

"Well, after the fact, I'm sorry. I think that's why we retell the old stories: they're *our* stories, smoothed over and softened by time." I wondered if other history buffs didn't get lost, too, and that's why they did it. "For a little bit, I can be someone else, made up of historic fact and my imagination," I said. "It's irresistible. I don't need a transporter or virtual reality to get there."

"Do you read historical fiction?"

"It's a good second choice. I don't mind taking a novelist's help to get into the past."

Tom looked far away. I wondered if he was thinking about Roxie and Bruce, or Armstrong and Libbie.

"Well, I'd like to get to know you better," I said, "but Dale is sick. I'd like to be just a friend, help you through this. I like Dale, even just knowing him a few days."

"I'm glad you're here, but I just can't get my mind off the old man."

Then he looked at me, really saw the person sitting opposite him. His eyes held me and made me dizzy. Then he leaned over and gave me a promissory note of a kiss.

We said good-bye and left for separate motels. I sighed as I steered down St. Michael's Drive, watching for my turn. The auspices weren't good, but Tom seemed to be nice, intelligent, caring. Now that he'd grown up.

I had to believe that something would work.

~

"Then I told him I couldn't stay any longer. If it was just me, that was one thing, but it was Clarence and Teresa and I didn't think it was right that they should have to be hurt," said the nurse's aide.

Dale reluctantly turned as I entered his hospital room the next morning.

"This here is Edna," Dale said. He looked at the woman as though she were a movie star. She was perhaps thirty, pudgy but firm, with shining black hair pulled back from her face. Her uniform fit like a crisp cotton slipcover and she wore a single elaborate silver ring. She was beautiful in her own way, I realized, and Dale saw that and treated her like a beauty. She responded, as I had, as Morgan had, as all the women must have. And that was what Dale wanted: their response. He knew it helped to hear their stories. It helped him to be of use and it helped them to find a listener.

"I guess I should be going," Edna said.

"Come back and tell me what you did after you left Flagstaff," Dale said.

Edna smiled. She stowed a basin in his bedside stand and bundled up linen. "I'll check on you later, Dale," she said.

"You must be better," I said. "You're at it again."

Dale just smiled. He seemed to wilt a little after Edna left. "You're still hanging around, Sis? I thought you'd be on your way back home, as far as the Cimarron Crossing by now."

"A friend of mine got sick and I decided to stick around. Besides, I still have some mad money I haven't spent on silver jewelry."

"I'm glad you did. Tom's too cool. You're good for him."

"I knew all along you were an old pimp."

Dale laughed until it turned into a cough.

"I noticed you had another lady telling you her life story."

"It's a doozy. Those TV soap operas don't tell the half of it. I lived a simple life, lucky I had a good wife since I was twenty-five. But these poor women! They get treated terrible."

"I bet your wife wasn't treated terrible."

Dale smiled. "Tell me what you did yesterday."

So I told about the trip to Chimayó and when Dale asked, I got the vial of dirt and rubbed a little on his hand.

"I feel like I ought to go back and put up a letter. You look so much better today I think my prayers were answered."

"I feel worlds better, and I hope the doc will spring me before I starve to death. They finally brought me real food this morning."

"But no carne adovada."

Dale shook his head.

Tom came into the hospital room. Watching him cross the room made my mouth go dry. He moved with taut grace, compact, muscular. His face was ordinary—his nose the same as Dale's: too big, too hooked. His pale eyes looked coldly on the world, until he smiled, then I felt warm.

"Edna was telling him the story of her life," I tattled.

"Dad!"

Dale raised a hand. "Now after a lady gave me a bath, I felt like I should get to know her."

"As long as you don't get too tired out."

But Dale already looked a little tired. It was an hour before lunch trays arrived and I didn't want to keep him talking. "You two go on ahead," Dale said. "I'm doing fine. Edna said she'd bring me my tray and tell me the rest of her story. After she ran away from that cowboy Cliff in Flagstaff, she lived in her car and worked cleaning houses for two months before she started working here. She's doing fine now and she's taking a class for her GED."

"I want a full report on the rest of the staff by tomorrow," I ordered.

Dale grinned and after a moment, Tom did, too. He had a sense of humor, I thought, with a five-second delay.

"Do you want to go somewhere?" I asked.

"I guess so." Tom hesitated.

"We could have lunch and drive to Ojo Caliente or up to Taos," I suggested.

"Why don't you two go to Puye and climb up. You've got the shoes for it, Sis."

I looked down at my Reeboks. Tom was wearing Nikes.

"What is it?" Tom asked.

"You go like you're going to Los Alamos, then there's a turn-off," said Dale. "Then you climb up the cliff to the top of this mesa. It'll do you good to get some exercise." He handed us the tourist guide.

CHAPTER TEN
PUYE MESA

~

*T*om and I stopped in Española for lunch at a restaurant with plain Formica tables and chairs and a minimum of trendy peach/turquoise decor. I saw two women in the open kitchen assemble our plates and the food tasted like two nice ladies had fixed it, and it was terrific.

When we got to Puye, we parked and walked through the visitor center where T-shirts and other items were for sale. It was on a reservation and had a laid-back feeling, much different from Park Service centers. Outside, a Madonna-faced woman sold miniature pottery items while her children played nearby. We looked up to see the ruins, a series of caves in the almost-vertical face of the tawny cliff. I wondered how old they were.

"Shall we?" I asked.

"Seems like the thing to do. Unless you want to drive around."

"That's not the point."

I led the way. Rounded steps had been cut so that a determined person could climb up. Handholds seemed to be where I needed them. Occasionally, only ladders would get us up another level. We looked in the little cave rooms and read the signs and I wondered what it would be like to live in the heart of the stone. The climb grew more vertical toward the top. I forgot that heights gave me vertigo until I made the mistake of looking down, then I was seized by the fear of falling. I grabbed the ladder and waited 'til my heart quit racing. Then I kept going, stubborn, determined, and didn't look down again until I was safely ten feet back from the edge at the top of the mesa.

I had concentrated on climbing with the cliff a foot in front of my face. Now, I looked around and my heart soared! I raised my arms and turned 360 degrees. To the north I saw so far that the horizon faded blue against the sky. A miracle! I turned, looked, turned, looked. Mountains, forest, distance. I got dizzy and had to stop.

"My heart is flying," I said and Tom smiled. We walked toward adobe ruins where teenage boys were cutting weeds.

A kiva open to non-Indians attracted visitors. There were perhaps a dozen people on top of the mesa, a couple of four-wheel-drive vehicles, and a pickup with lawn tools. I wondered if they had to deconsecrate a kiva before outsiders could go in. We wandered around the ruins, studying the shape and arrangement of the buildings. I couldn't wipe the smile off my face. Dale had sent us on a trip to the top of the world. We didn't talk. What I was seeing and feeling bypassed thinking. I hoped Tom felt the same.

After we walked around the ruins, we sat near the north edge and gazed into the distances at the landscape—violet, rose, amber, and amethyst.

Tom put his arm around me and I fitted into the hollow. We didn't say anything, didn't need to say anything for long minutes. Then Tom sang softly, "On a clear day..." until he ran out of words, then he hummed through to the end of a verse. Nobody had ever sung to me before.

I was delighted in a way I had never been before. Singing a song was something foolish, high school, dramatic. Non-rational, even. Feeling him breathe, feeling the vibrations through his ribs, went straight into my nervous system. I saw him, heard him, felt him. Smelled the faint aftershave he favored, longed to taste him.

I didn't want this moment to stop. I wanted to feel high and turned-on and protected forever. And I wanted something more.

Tom turned and smoothed my tumbled hair off my face and cradled my cheeks in his hands. He leaned forward to kiss me. I thought my body would rise up from where I sat, I was so happy. We kissed softly, as children kiss, then more seriously, then really seriously. He shifted so both arms went around me, then we were kneeling face to face on the rocky ground with our bodies pressed together. I embraced hard muscle, bone, and desire. Tom made a low growl, half pain, half passion, and pushed me back on the dry, crackling grass. He lay on top, his mouth fastened to mine. I was embarrassed, but I didn't care. I tasted, drank, drowned.

When he stopped for breath I said, "We can't here."

He was panting, but forced himself up. His eyes locked mine and I felt that invisible basin inside my pelvis fill. He stroked my face and neck. I discovered his ears were ticklish. He cupped one breast and I sobbed. Then he remembered where we were.

"I guess we better stop," he said and I kissed him, kissed his clavicle through his shirt, kissed his neck, kissed his eyes.

"We've got to stop," I said. But I couldn't release him.

"We can't make a spectacle of ourselves in public," he said and wrapped both arms around me.

"Really tacky," I agreed and twined my legs with his.

"People making an exhibition of themselves." He rubbed the length of my thigh. "Vulgar."

"Those kids raking grass are probably getting hot," I said.

He looked over, sighed, and reluctantly stopped. My heart was a helium balloon. My legs didn't want to work right. We walked to the edge of the cliff.

"Do you want to go down the long way, on the road?"

I hesitated. "Naw, I can do it."

"Of course you can."

Still we hesitated.

"I feel free," I said. "I feel light and free. I can almost fly."

"This is that feeling I used to get when I was inside the music," Tom said. He kissed me softly.

～

It was slow going down. I stopped often to look over the landscape. It was too beautiful to miss and the vertigo stayed away. I could see a smudge I thought was Santa Fe and the snake of black highway across the land.

"It's so beautiful," I said over and over.

When we got to my car, Tom said, "Let's go to my room."

And I nodded because I couldn't speak.

When we got back to Tom's motel on Cerrillos Road, I parked and we hurried through the lavish lobby hand in hand. Champagne, not blood, ran in my veins. But when Tom opened the door to his room, I could see the light blinking on the phone. We both knew, but he called and confirmed.

"Dad is gone."

～

"Will you take me to the hospital?" Tom asked stiffly. The armor that had dissolved on Puye Mesa was hardening into place again.

"Sure. Why don't I see if I can run errands or make phone calls?"

"I'll be perfectly all right," he said.

"Maybe I can help."

We drove in silence to the hospital.

I could scarcely believe it was Dale. This corpse was a yellow, shrunken old man, not Dale—all gab and a yard wide. Tom stood in front of him and stared. After a time, he reached out and touched the cheek. Tears ran down my face. I walked out into the hall.

It had been too recent, too hard. Six months and all the pain was fresh. Hard tears forced their way out painfully. This death sent me back to my father's death. I felt the loss again, I was abandoned again. I leaned against the corridor wall and sobbed. Dale's good humor and the way he called me "Sis" and his smile—gone. I couldn't live a long time because every death would remind me of deaths that had gone before and the weight of the sadness would be too much to carry.

I sat while Tom phoned a mortuary and arranged for cremation. He agreed to an autopsy. He signed papers the nursing secretary presented to him.

"Are you going to have a memorial service in Independence?" I asked.

"I thought I'd just scatter his ashes here." Tom looked washed out and his eyes were almost colorless.

"His friends need to say good-bye."

"I don't have his little black book with me," Tom snapped.

"Can you remember any names? There's a grapevine that'll spread the word, I'm sure."

Tom opened Dale's billfold and spread slips of paper on the table.

"Senior citizen stuff. I never kept it all straight."

"A week from Saturday?"

"I suppose."

"Where? Did he belong to a church?"

"Englewood Baptist, I think."

"Why don't you talk to the people from the funeral home and I'll take care of this part."

Tom got up and paced around the little table. He looked like an android, almost lifelike, programmed to follow directions. I pulled the phone over and got a notebook out of my purse. I set a time and place with the church secretary.

"Next Saturday, eleven A.M.," I told Tom when he returned. I flipped pages in the notebook. "Flowers?"

"Would you stop?" Tom's voice was gritty with rage.

The notebook fell from my hands. "Of course." What had happened with the funeral home director? What was wrong? Was it becoming real?

"Why are you being so managerial? Quit sucking up to me!"

"Just trying to help." The words hurt. I would relinquish all responsibility, if that was what he wanted. "I need some dinner," I said. "How about you?"

"I don't need dinner! I don't need for you to tell me to eat dinner! I can handle this myself. Leave me alone!"

He turned my helpfulness back on me and slammed me for it.

"Do you want the information about the memorial service?"

"There's not going to be any service."

"Too late. The phone tree is activated."

"I'm not carrying the ashes back in my car!"

"His friends need some sort of ceremony. So do I."

"You hardly knew him."

"The same goes for you."

Tom looked stunned and for a moment I thought he would burst into tears. He had the vulnerable, hurt look of a small boy. Then his face hardened. "Get out! I've had enough of your interference."

"You're ashamed!" I said. "We were on Puye Mesa feeling good, ready to get it on and have a good time. It's guilt and shame and embarrassment. We were doing kissy-face the moment he died. You can't handle that!"

"Slut! You'd fuck your way into my life. You've been Miss Congeniality since we met."

He struck the table with both fists and I jumped. "Pretending you're some history scholar. Ingratiating yourself with my father. Wheedling your way into our lives!" His face was nearly purple. Bits of saliva sprayed. "Get out!"

I ripped pages out of my notebook and threw all the paper on the table. "Phone the church if you want to cancel the service."

I couldn't bring Dale back from the dead. But I thought I could make it up to the universe, which kept track of all my sins. I would be helpful and that would take care of the bad timing this afternoon, for all the good, high feelings at Puye.

I remembered another time when I felt bad at that Christmas dinner at Grandma Zita's.

❧

Usually Christmas dinner with my family meant Bing Crosby singing, a turkey and spaghetti, real pies, not Tippin's, and kids running amok through the upstairs bedrooms. Everybody ate too much because we were all good cooks.

After dinner the girl cousins and the aunts and I were cleaning up the kitchen. Allison, a cousin who also attended Kansas University, announced that Kevin and I were living together.

"What is she talking about?" Mama's face darkened and her eyes stormed. It was a face that had frightened me into telling the truth all my life.

"Kevin and I share an apartment." I tried to sound calm.

"Why didn't you tell your father or me?"

"Because I didn't want to have to go through this!" I was angry and betrayed and ashamed. The emotions cancelled each other out and I didn't know what I felt.

I turned to Ally. "Why don't you keep your big mouth shut?"

"Just because he's big and blond and gorgeous—" Ally began.

"Are you ashamed to bring him to dinner?" Aunt Sophie asked. "We'd like to meet him."

"Slut!" said Aunt Catherine. "Don't you know he'll never buy the cow if he's getting the milk free?"

"Thanks for comparing me to a milk cow," I snapped.

"When did this start?" asked Grandma Zita softly. Her eyes looked sad.

"This fall. We've known each other a year. He's beautiful. We're going to get married when we graduate."

"He'll never marry you now," said Aunt Catherine. Aunt Catherine's daughter was so homely she couldn't give it away.

"I don't need any nineteenth-century Sicilian morality," I said. I was sweating, crying, and as mad as I had ever allowed myself to be with someone in the family. I dropped the damp dishtowel and stalked out of the kitchen. Papa Tony's eyes looked questions. "Later, okay Dad?" I grabbed my coat and drove almost to St. Joe before I calmed down. Then I drove back home and faced my parents.

~

I got down to the lobby of the hospital and out to my car and found a restaurant open, then drove to my motel in the waning dusk. I mechanically packed my bags and asked for a wake-up call. I had closed the curtains against the late summer dusk and now stuck my Walkman headphones on, but music couldn't stop Tom's voice shouting in my head. I cried, even moaned. Cried for Dale, for Tom lost to me, for my father, for Antonia, for all my sins. When I could keep moving I was okay. It felt like freedom and nothing could bother me, but I'd stopped in Santa Fe and everything had caught up with me, including the lead jacket. No escape velocity for memories.

I tried to concentrate on the newspaper, but anything that happened when I was on vacation always seemed unreal. Stories in the Santa Fe *New Mexican* about environmental problems and legal battles over water rights and a conference defending the honor of

Kit Carson seemed even more removed. I'd give the Santa Fe Opera a miss. When I took a trip and read the local papers, I realized how narrow my world was—work and family and a modest social life. I had never visited Europe, hadn't known where Serbia was until I saw the maps on CNN. Usually I felt stupid because I didn't care about anything that didn't affect me personally. Israel and Haiti and North Korea were abstract and unreal. Only people's suffering touched me. Then I saw a story on an inside page reminding parents that Sudden Infant Death Syndrome could be prevented if babies were put to sleep on their backs. Oh God, not that.

Mom said one summer when I was little, Elvis died when we were on a family vacation. She'd always had trouble believing it really happened. *National Enquirer* still wasn't convinced. I wouldn't remember these headlines. This would be the vacation when I met Dale and Tom, and Dale died in Santa Fe.

Before, whenever I took a trip, I had to go back home. This time there was no job waiting. I had a little money saved. I would keep moving, keep the car pointed away from Kansas City.

I thought of the plastic vial of Chimayó dirt in my bag. I knelt beside the motel bed and prayed.

Tom lashed out, yes, but he hadn't known the single most cutting word: slut. That was Aunt Catherine's word. Dad's cousin Rose preferred "living in sin." Grandma Zita wept silently. Mama didn't call names, she just did guilt trips.

This was the sixth day since I left Kansas City.

❦

The next morning Tom found me at the McDonald's near my motel eating breakfast. The dry biscuit stuck in my throat. I wanted to tell him off, wanted to condole, wanted to hit and kick, wanted to pretend he wasn't there.

"I'm sorry, what I said," he mumbled. He didn't look particularly contrite.

"Fine."

"I behaved badly and I'm sorry," he said.

"Right."

"You're not making it easy."

"Sorry."

"Those were real tears you shed."

"Right."

"I did feel ashamed. Because of the timing. I feel bad about how I treated you."

"That's fine." Why was I letting him off? I felt like a punch-drunk fighter who gets slugged every time he gets up off the mat. I felt mean and aggressive: "I'm glad we were up there, at Puye Mesa," I said. "We climbed up, like kids, and we were happy. We could see for miles. You sang me a song. I was free and high and light. We held each other and kissed. That was great. Don't forget Dale sent us there. Dale wanted us to be happy. That was his gift to us."

Tom frowned, as though he disagreed. I was tired of talking. The locals had cleared out and tourists streamed in. The sun's horizontal rays bleached color and the air was clear and still cool. Cars droned on the street outside and the electronic voices of the drive-through spoke undecipherable code.

He shifted his feet and looked uncomfortable standing. I didn't ask him to sit.

"This morning after the cremation, I'm taking the ashes up in the mountains," said Tom. "Your simplistic prayers at Chimayó didn't work. I'll turn off there for the High Road to Taos."

"There's a big pull-out near Truchas, about halfway up. The view should be spectacular." I crossed myself. Eternal rest be granted him. I waited, hoping Tom was done.

"I want to apologize."

"You did."

"Well, can we spend some time together?"

"I don't think so."

"I'm sorry I was hard on you."

"I'm not. Now I know how you really feel about me."

"That's not fair."

I shrugged.

"We can get together later."

"Go away. Leave me alone." I felt too weary to talk.

"You never told me your story."

That stopped me. I never told anybody my story. But he had listened to my history stories and told me his own. Maybe I owed him one. It would surely put him off me for good.

"What are you really like?" he asked.

"If you knew, you wouldn't like me. I was an unwed mother."

"That's not unusual anymore."

"Well, in my family it was a mortal sin. I fell in love with a pretty face."

"Tell me."

I took a deep breath, but it didn't help. Could I sit in this bright and impersonal place and bring back that painful story? I didn't think this one would unroll as easily as Libbie and Armstrong's or Lizzie Simpson's. I nodded and Tom sat down.

"Kevin and I were both students in the computer science department at KU. I was working there." My old cubicle jumped into mind and I could see the calendar, the cabinets, and my desktop with Gumby and Pokey on top of the monitor. "Kevin finally noticed me. He was so drop-dead good looking I couldn't think of anything but yes."

"Was that what made you fall in love?" Tom asked.

"He was six foot two, muscles, blond hair, a face like a movie star. I felt good just looking at him. Here I am, I look okay—short and if I don't watch it, I'll look like one of my dumpy aunts. Italian nose, curly hair. Women would go up to Kevin in bars and give him their business cards, their car keys."

༞ ✿ ༞

LAWRENCE

That first night we went to a place on Massachusetts Avenue. Kevin's hard muscle under smooth skin. Smell of aftershave. Kevin's voice made me vibrate. We laughed a lot that night. I learned he was from California, and planned to return. After a couple of beers, he suggested we go out to this trestle he knew about and wait 'til a train came over. I had heard of students playing on the tracks and sometimes hopping freights. I told myself I didn't have to do anything. I floated on a cloud of desire, helped a little by the beer.

We drove west out of Lawrence and parked off a farm road. Kevin led me to a trestle that carried a pair of tracks over a creek. We stood on the tracks and looked down through the ties and vertigo hit me. I backed to firm ground.

Kevin said, "Let's just sit underneath for a while."

We went below the trestle and necked on the grass, seeking, exploring, and sighing. It was a golden evening in early autumn. Cottonwoods and hickories were just turning. Wind made the brushy woods rustle, and branches bobbed in the wind. The rich, decaying odor of dead leaves mixed with the dry grass, which smelled like a new broom.

"Can you hear it?" Kevin asked.

"Hear what?" Then I caught the faint hissing of the tracks.

Kevin pulled me up and led me under the trestle. The noise was getting louder.

"Stay behind this girder," he said. "You'll be safe here. The train will go by and you press your body into these metal ribs. The train's over you, you can't get hurt, but it'll be a rush."

I pressed myself into place, clung to the metal braces. He pressed himself against me, holding me safe. He was hard, excited. I was scared and excited, too. The rumble of the train got louder and louder, then it burst across the trestle and the wind hit and the trestle vibrated and I thought I would fly off. The train passed a few feet above. The sound was indescribable. Kevin hollered. The metal sang and shook. My lungs vibrated and my bones trembled. Then the train was across and the throbbing stilled and the happy noise of the train faded.

I shook with fear and adrenaline, unbearably excited.

We climbed off the trestle and he laid me back gently in the warm dry grass. Afterward I said, "Let's go to my place." That weekend we made love day and night. I would go out of my head, lose track of time, forget where I was.

"Where are you?" he'd ask.

"Here I am," I'd gasp. "Here I am." And we'd do it again.

That weekend we ate everything in my fridge. We couldn't look at each other without laughing. Kevin left once, came back with beer and a pizza. I said he could move in. It seemed the only thing to do. He had his good points. One month when I warned him I had PMS, he made a huge comfort meal—meatloaf, mashed potatoes and gravy, tapioca pudding. Then he rubbed my back until I fell asleep. I woke up in time for the ten o'clock news and we made love slowly, gently. I orgasmed once and he held himself back until I came again and again. I was so naive I hadn't known I could keep doing it.

We only had one fight. I wanted to go out with him for a beer one night some time in October and he snapped at me, "I need my own space; I need room to breathe, understand?"

I shrugged and decided I could use a break myself. After that, he went out at odd times and I didn't think anything of it until I saw him coming out of a place on Massachusetts one afternoon with a slim blond girl who looked sort of familiar.

"Who's she?" I asked later, hiding my jealousy, I thought, by sounding casual.

"What?" Kevin said.

"The girl. The blonde. On Mass. last night."

He looked blandly at me and said, "Kim. From my history seminar. A bunch of us went out afterward. She's from LA, too, so we were doing 'do you knows.'"

He graduated in December and planned to check out his job in LA over the holidays. I would finish in May and join him.

I felt like I'd had some low-grade flu for a couple of weeks around Thanksgiving, then I didn't get my period. It was just before I went home for Christmas break. Kevin didn't want to meet my parents. A couple of days before he left for California, I stopped at Osco and bought a kit.

It was positive. I was happy that night when I told him. I thought he would be happy, or at least pleasantly surprised, but he leaped up and turned on me in a rage. "You can't be pregnant! Who else have you been sleeping with? It's not my baby."

I was shocked. "Of course it's yours. I haven't been with anyone else since we started going together. You are *wrong*, evil to think this of me."

"Get rid of it. It isn't too late?"

"I don't want an abortion. I thought we were getting married. This will just make it happen a little sooner."

"I'm not marrying a slut!"

"Slut? What are you talking about?" I was dismayed, hurt, and puzzled.

"You can't prove it's mine! I'll never pay child support. You can't strap me with this. I'm not ready."

I was crying, from rage and hurt. "I thought you loved me!"

He didn't answer. He stormed into the bedroom, kicked some stuff around. I sat stunned, unable to think.

After a while he came out and stood in front of me. "I'll drive you to the Overland Park clinic," he said. "You won't have trouble getting rid of it. I'll pay for it."

I said nothing. I wasn't a strong Catholic, but abortion was wrong for me.

"Be reasonable!" he shouted.

I looked at Kevin then and saw something I hadn't noticed before: a scared little boy. With no emotional depth. I was sorry this wasn't working out, but glad I was seeing past my lust and his blond good looks. I had nestled in his uncommon beauty, making the usual error of thinking anyone who looked that marvelous had to be a good person. Under the pretty exterior, he was more self-centered than most men, since he'd always gotten what he wanted from women.

"Get out." My voice didn't sound like I meant it. I cleared my throat, stood up, and walked over to the bookcase, where I steadied myself. "Get out. Never speak to me again."

"If you try to prove it's my kid, I'll take you to court. It'll be real messy." He sounded vicious. "You're not hitting me with child support."

"Haven't you heard of DNA testing?" I taunted. "Don't worry. I don't want him to ever know you were his father." I took a deep breath. "My lawyer will be ready for any messiness you care to start. Get out."

This time I must have sounded like I meant it.

He looked relieved. I stood there, knees trembling, holding onto the bookcase while he threw his clothes into his bags.

"I'll come back for the books."

He came back the next day, apologized, and said he would send for me when he found a job, and that we could patch it up. He left for California and I went home for Christmas, that terrible Christmas when Aunt Catherine called me a slut. That seemed to be everyone's favorite word. And they hadn't even known I was pregnant.

After Christmas I waited, but Kevin didn't phone. I called the number he gave me, left messages, but got no answer. I tried a telegram. The semester started and still nothing from Kevin. I tried phoning at different times of day and always got his answering machine: "Hi, I can't come to the phone right now, but let me hear from you." Even his phony sincerity made my heart race.

Then one day, just before Valentine's Day, almost two months after he left, a woman answered the phone. "This is Kim."

"Let me talk to Kevin," I managed to get out. "What's going on?" I asked him.

"Uh, well, Kim decided to move back here."

"Are you living together?" I didn't want to believe it.

"Uh, well, sort of."

"What about me? About us?"

"Well, you didn't want an abortion and I need my space. I didn't know what else to do but split. Sorry."

I hung up. I stood hollow. I wasn't entitled to anger. I'd asked for this.

That night I cried until I made myself sick.

The next Friday night when I finished at the Information Systems building, I drove the thirty-odd miles home to Kansas City. I told my parents and listened while my mother raged. Movie stars and teenagers and career women had babies out of wedlock. My family's Sicilian morality could still be harsh and judgmental.

"I can't bear it!" Mama buried her face in her hands. She had stormed for exactly half an hour. "I have a migraine headache from this. Don't show your face here again. I have nothing more to say to you. Ever." She slammed her bedroom door dramatically.

I went into the bathroom until I quit shaking.

"Dad, I need your help," I said when I came out.

"Anything, sweetie." Papa Tony smiled his sad-eyed smile. When did his hair get this white next to his golfer's tanned face? His generous nose looked elegant and his brown eyes deep.

"I'm sorry. I was in love. I thought we were getting married."

"I'm just sorry you got hurt." And he really looked as though he meant it. With his sympathy to soften me, I wept like a little girl.

"I don't want anything to happen to my own flesh and blood," he said. "Either of you."

The baby was already real for him. It wasn't just a shameful condition.

"You find a good doctor in Lawrence, you hear? Or find a doctor here and have the baby back here."

"I don't think Mama wants me back here."

"This is always your home. She's just upset today."

"It's not due 'til after graduation. I'll keep working at Information Systems."

"Whatever you say, sweetie," he said. He rested his hand on my head and it was a blessing. I knew he'd be there when I needed him.

I looked around the franchise restaurant, filled with vacationing families and bright children. Happy people out to have a good time.

"So I'm a slut. And an unwed mother. That's my story. I can sympathize with you over your ex-wife, sympathize with you over Roxie—we're the brotherhood of the betrayed." I moved the napkin and water glass and fiddled with the plastic fork on my tray. "All the history stories are *my* stories. Falling in love, being jealous, being hurt, having a baby. There are just a few stories, Willa Cather said, and we keep repeating them as fiercely as though they have never been told."

"You never mentioned a baby before. Who's taking care of it?"

"Oh, God." When I remembered holding Antonia for the first time, I was happy again. My heart soared. I couldn't help but smile. But I had never talked about what came next. Wasn't sure I could. Here was my chance to get it all out.

"No reason to keep it a secret," Tom said.

"I was ashamed I had been dumb and trusted Kevin. I was ashamed I'd been so careless I'd gotten pregnant. I was sorry I'd worried my parents. I was not sorry, not *ever*, not ashamed, not regretful about Antonia." I rushed into the story before I scared myself out of it.

"So I finished classes and graduated, then moved back home. Papa Tony took me to the hospital when it was time. Medically uneventful, but of course, the most important event in my life. Thank God memories of labor fade."

"It's a girl," somebody said. They suctioned and the baby cried, first a kitten squeak, then a full-fledged cry. They cut the cord then wrapped the baby up and plopped her on my still-swollen belly. The baby raged at what had happened and cried steadily. I held her and thought I would burst with joy. I wiped blood and vernix off the tiny face with one shaking finger. She stopped crying and rooted toward the finger, investigating. I wept, grateful and exuberant.

I felt the placenta pass. They took the baby to weigh and to do Apgar tests. They cleaned her up, then wrapped her like a tiny mummy and put her in a crib.

Papa was waiting in my room. "Are you okay?" he asked softly.

"Best day of my life," I said.

Then the nurse brought him a gown and mask and wheeled the baby in.

"Do you have a name?" the nurse asked.

"Yes. Antonia Brancato."

Tears came to Papa's eyes.

My mother had sworn she wouldn't look at the bastard. I dreaded another scene.

"Don't worry," my dad said before he left. "I told her what happened and she couldn't stand it. She had to come."

"She's beautiful," Mama said. "When can you bring her home?"

"Are you sure you want a crying baby?" I asked.

"It's my grandbaby!" my mother replied, as if that settled it.

"Come and see what I did," said Mama when we got home the next day. She led me to the spare bedroom. When I left Tuesday morning, it had held the sewing machine and other junk that accumulated between guests. It now featured fresh paint, new pink curtains, and a fuzzy area rug under the new white wicker crib. A matching dresser overflowed with washed and folded baby clothes. Boxes of Pampers were stacked in the corner. A new rocking chair stood nearby. A bird mobile hung over the crib.

I handed Antonia to her grandmother. "I think you should do the honors," I said. Mama looked ecstatic as she took the little bundle. She murmured baby talk as she laid the baby in the crib and unwrapped each layer until she found a damp diaper. Antonia cooed and kicked with the pleasure of being free. She was in good hands, the best.

In a couple of days, Antonia's red newborn face quit looking squashed and she smelled like heaven. Mama could scarcely stand to hand her to me.

They never mentioned Kevin, or anything about the situation. Antonia redeemed me in their eyes.

I knew the life of a single parent would be difficult, but other women did it. And I had a perfect, beautiful baby whom I loved beyond reason.

I couldn't wait to begin my new career. Antonia and I would move into an apartment the first of September. By mid-August I had been back at work for a month, driving from North Kansas City around the belt highway to Sprint offices in a southern suburb. The baby gained weight, nursed voraciously. My figure was very slowly returning to normal. My parents didn't want us to leave, although I thought they looked tired. I treasured those dark, quiet times in the middle of the night when I fed the tiny baby. I was learning that Antonia had a personality of her own, her own funny yawn, her own scowl, her own way of patting my finger before she grasped it. I was glad Mama could watch Antonia while I worked, and I wished I could stay home.

Everything happened fast. A Friday night in August, Mama and my dad went to an old movie. I put on an old T-shirt and shorts. I fed Antonia, then filled the baby tub for a bath. Antonia stared at me, studied my face with dark-blue baby eyes. Antonia knew the difference between me and Mama. She had one cry for unhappiness and one to get attention. I stroked the fuzz of baby hair. I talked as I soaped the fine baby skin. Nothing felt better than a baby's skin and nothing smelled better than a clean baby. Antonia sneezed when I put a soap bubble on her nose.

After she was dressed and warm, Antonia fussed, so I rocked her until she fell asleep. She was breathing with her mouth open and I hoped she wasn't catching a cold. I put her in her wicker bed and went back into the living room to watch the ten o'clock news. I was so tired I dozed off sitting up, then woke as the program finished.

The intercom from the crib had been silent. I got up to go to bed myself and went in to look at Antonia, for that necessary pleasure of watching my child sleeping.

She wasn't breathing.

I couldn't believe it. It couldn't have been twenty minutes. I hadn't heard a sound.

Frantically, I picked her up, closed the nostrils, and covered her tiny mouth with my own. I carried the still form to the phone and punched 911, gave the address between breaths. I knew I had to keep calm, keep breathing.

My parents returned at the same time the paramedics arrived.

The efficient young man and woman took the infant, covered her face with an oxygen mask, and radioed the hospital. I sat with her in the back of the ambulance while they tried to resuscitate her as we raced to the hospital.

I did not want to give Antonia up at the emergency room. I listened, hyper-alert, to noises, muffled voices, orders. But I knew.

After half an hour, the doctor came out looking defeated. Her long auburn hair looked messy and her lipstick was gone. Her stethoscope hung out of the pocket of her lab coat. The woman shook her head. "I'm sorry."

My legs gave out and I sat abruptly in the waiting room chair. I burst into tears, and the doctor wrapped her arms around my heaving shoulders. I cried and thought I would die myself. This wasn't fair! I'd done the right things, I had gotten through the hard parts. I'd worked and done everything I was supposed to. My parents arrived and we cried together. I signed papers I was too numb to read and my parents took me home. It felt very late. My mother looked stunned. I had never seen Papa Tony look so sad. We persuaded Mama to take a Valium and go to bed.

My aunt Catherine came over at eight o'clock the next morning, fixed breakfast, and started making phone calls. She arranged for a Mass of the Resurrection and worked out details with the funeral home. She stayed on the phone all morning, calling relatives, doing the necessary things.

I kept forgetting what I was doing. I phoned my boss, explained what had happened, and said I wouldn't be in the next week. Family emergency.

There was a funeral. There were lots of people there, all the family who lived in town. The flowers were beautiful. I did what people told me to do and I got through it. The following Monday morning I went to work. My mother said it was a mistake, but I knew if I didn't have something to occupy me, I'd go crazy or never stop crying.

And I did get through each day, concentrating on the job at hand, putting one foot in front of the other. I was correct and polite, but people left me alone, as though grief were contagious. I didn't care. I moved into the new apartment, leaving the baby stuff at my mother's. I told my mother I was going out with girlfriends so she wouldn't worry about me staying home all the time. I joined the Westerners' Posse and one Civil War Roundtable and the Trails Association and went to stodgy dinner meetings where I learned a lot of history. The meetings kept me from being sucked completely into my new job, which seemed to demand more energy, more concentration than I had. That was all right. I wanted to concentrate on something outside myself.

I felt like my mind didn't function. I couldn't think. I'd slip up, forget things, and leave things out. Then Papa Tony had his heart attack, and died. And I got fired. Too much in one year.

The past faded. Tom studied my face.

"When I met you I thought it might be the start of some kind of normal life," I said. "Whoever in the Universe regulates traffic in my life dumped too much at once." I remembered the hours of lead, trying to work, befuddled by grief. I thought I was handling it. I worked long hours, kept busy at home, volunteered weekends, frantic and exhausted, but grief ruled just the same. "I should have gone to a doctor and let him put me in the hospital. I'd have gotten a month's insurance and been officially ill, mentally ill, but I tried to handle it on my own and got fired. I'm on a permanent vacation. I don't have to go back." I placed my hands flat on the table. "That's my story."

Tom said nothing. He looked at me with a neutral, interested expression. He said, "You were trying to be Aunt Catherine for me."

"Yeah, I guess I was." I picked up my purse, stood, tipped my tray into the trash, and walked outside. The day was warming up.

"Go with me to scatter the ashes."

"No, thanks."

"Meet me later. Let's start again."

"No. I don't want to."

I felt loose and exhausted, as though I'd cleared my brain of toxic waste. I'd told the story I kept locked inside, but I didn't want to deal with Tom, didn't want to see the knowing expression on his face when I mentioned my past.

I got in my car and headed west. I felt like an untethered balloon. My vacation down the Santa Fe Trail had overlapped Dale's itinerary, and I had projected a fantasy on Tom and when it fell apart, couldn't get my bearings. What had I wanted to do when I left Kansas City? Drive west. I could live anywhere I found a campground. I could motor in a leisurely fashion, stop when I wanted to drink from the history well. Study, learn, see. Let the big western sky stretch my mind.

I drove south on I-25, then picked up I-40 in Albuquerque. Too many cars going too fast in too many lanes. I didn't stop 'til I reached Grants, where I studied Indian jewelry in the store windows after lunch.

I rolled through the incomparable landscape, thinking of Navajos and medicine men and what I could remember from a course in anthropology. I'd find Fort Whipple and remember Martha Summerhayes, my favorite army wife.

CHAPTER ELEVEN
CAMP VERDE / FORT WHIPPLE

~

*F*lagstaff was high and cool and I resisted the pull of the great canyon. I wanted serene history, no tourists or eco-angst, so I continued to Prescott.

The vast landscape calmed me. Maybe it calmed the army wives, made Susan Magoffin brave, gave Lizzie Simpson hope. Martha Summerhayes missed it the rest of her life. It must have seemed like an extended holiday to some of them—riding, hunting, living rough.

Something flickered at the edges of my consciousness. What would I do next? I ignored it, found something else to think about. I wanted to keep driving, keep moving. That way nothing could catch me.

Martha Summerhayes had lived in Ehrenberg, on the Colorado River, the western border of Arizona. She had traveled to Fort Whipple, which was now a VA hospital in Prescott. She wrote of her naked Cocopah butler in Ehrenberg with a rare sense of humor.

I drove past the hospital and went on into Prescott until I found a motel. I needed to stretch and walk. Prescott was an old mining town and the city's main drag snaked along the side of a steep canyon. After eating, I drove back to the hospital. I had to imagine the fort and the parade grounds, but the duplex Victorian houses marched sedately around the edge of the complex, as they had when Mrs. Aldrich welcomed Martha to Fort Whipple.

I sat on a bench on the hospital grounds. The sun headed behind the mountains. I wished I had someone to tell the story to. If I said it out loud, all the emotions seemed easier to handle.

Mattie's letters home told her story.

Arizona Territory
1876
   Dear Mama and Papa:
   I know that when I arrived home I was so ill you despaired for me and that I vowed never to return to Arizona Territory, but since the birth of Katherine and since I have regained my health, I feel equal to the hardships of a frontier garrison.
   I feel I must explain why I did not heed your pleas to remain on Nantucket and why I have turned my back on the comfort of the old house. I know I complained endlessly of the lack of amenities in Arizona and how difficult it was to keep house, but in the East I discovered that I am truly a soldier's wife, and must come back to it all.
   God willing, I will not have to repeat that terrible journey when we left Camp Apache with two government ambulances, two army wagons, and a Mexican guide. Jack had been ordered back from Ehrenberg, which was a shipping point on the Colorado River, and we traveled through the northern mountains

of the Territory to Fort Whipple before going on. Harry
was scarcely three months old and I wore a pistol belt
around my waist.

Our first stop was Cooley's ranch, where his wife
and another Indian woman, both tidy and good-
looking, prepared us a most wholesome and appetizing
supper. After we ate, I sat sleepily, gazing at the fire
in the corner. "Jack," I whispered, "which girl do you
think is Cooley's wife?"

"I don't know," he answered. "Both of them, I
guess."

I had a difficult time, in those days, reconciling
reality with what I had been taught was right, and I
had to sort over my ideas and deep-rooted prejudices
a good many times. The few white men led respectable
lives in that country. The standard was not high, but
when I thought of the dreary years they had already
spent there and the years they must look forward to
remaining there, I was willing to reserve my judgment.

The next segment of our trip was over malpais, which
was lava beds. There was no trace of a road. A few
hours of this grinding and crunching over crushed lava
wearied us all, and the animals found it hard pulling,
although the country was level.

Mrs. Bailey had her year-old boy with her, and we
experienced the utmost inconvenience from the lack
of warm water and other things necessary for the health
and comfort of the children. One night we rinsed their
towels in cold, hard well-water at Stinson's camp and
the two lieutenants stood and held the wet items before
the campfire until they were dry. I looked at them,
too tired to move, and thought about the uniform,
associated in my mind with brilliant functions—guard

mount, parades, and full-dress weddings. As I sat
gazing, they turned around and, realizing how almost
ludicrous they looked, began to laugh.

"Nice work for United States officers! Hey, Bailey,"
said Jack.

"It might be worse." The handsome Bailey sighed.

We continued the next day and stopped at the site of
old Camp Supply. That night wildcats flew in the
unglazed windows of our adobes, our dogs gave chase,
the babies began to cry, and Jack threw his boots and
scared the cats away. After momentary silence we tried
to sleep, but back came the cats and it began again.
Mrs. Bailey and I sat up all night with our poor babies.
At dawn our nerves were at a tension and our strength
gone—poor preparation for the day to follow.

Early the next day, we met a man who said he had
been fired upon by some Indians at Sanford's Pass.
We didn't pay much attention to his story. Soon after,
we passed an adobe ruin out of which crept two
bare-headed Mexicans so badly frightened that their
faces were pallid. They talked with the guide and
gesticulated, pointing to the pass. They had been fired
at and their ponies taken by some roving Apaches.
We gave them food and drink and they implored us,
by the Holy Virgin, not to go through the pass.

But the men took counsel and decided to go through.
Jack examined his revolver and saw that my pistol was
loaded. For miles, we strained our eyes, looking in the
direction whence the Mexican men had come.

I obeyed orders and lay in the bottom of the
ambulance. I took my derringer out of the holster and
cocked it. I looked at my little boy lying helpless there
beside me and at his delicate temples, lined with thin

blue veins, and wondered if I could follow the instructions I had received, for Jack had said, after the decision was made to go through the pass: "Now, Mattie, I don't think for a minute that there are any Injuns in that Pass, and you must not be afraid. We have got to go through it anyway. But . . ." He hesitated. "We may be mistaken. There may be a few of them in there, and they'll have a mighty good chance to get in a shot or two. And now listen: if I'm hit, you'll know what to do. You have your derringer. When you see that there is no help for it, if they get away with the whole outfit, why, there's only one thing to be done. Don't let them get the baby, for they will carry you both off and—well, you know the squaws are much more crueler than the bucks. Don't let them get either of you alive. Now"—to the driver—"go on."

After a bit, I took the gun off the cock and hoped I wouldn't have to act on Jack's directions.

From the first moment I set foot in Arizona, with the poisonous reptiles and prickly desert plants, the snakes and flying insects, I had not known real peace. Besides the vicissitudes of the environment, there was the ever-present threat of hostile Indians. True, at some garrisons the danger was slight, but it was never absent and in this instance, it could not have been stronger. I hardly remember a time during the years we were there when I was not in fear of some immediate peril, or in dread of some danger that threatened.

You may ask, Mama and Papa, if it was so difficult and filled with terror, why have I returned to it? I can only answer that somehow the hardships and deprivations which we have endured lose their bitterness when they have become only a memory.

I lay in that ambulance, thinking of you, my dear parents, and my brothers and sisters. I kept my eyes upon Jack's face. There he sat, rifle in hand, his features motionless, his eyes keenly watching out from one side of the ambulance, while a cavalryman, carbine in hand, watched the other side of the narrow canyon. The driver kept his animals steady and we rattled along.

At last I perceived the steep slope of the road. I looked out and saw that the Pass was widening. "Keep still," said Jack, without moving a feature. My heart seemed to stop beating and I dared not move again until I heard him say, "Thank God we're out of it! Get up, Mattie. See the river? We'll cross it and then we'll be out of their damned country!"

When we stopped that night, and the other ambulance drove up alongside of us, Ella Bailey and I looked at each other. We did not talk, but I believe we cried just a little.

We headed for Sunset Crossing, a romantic name for a wild place. When we got there, the river was up and the guide said there was much quicksand. The ford had changed since last he saw it, so we did not try to cross that night. After the tents were pitched, I heated some water until it was warm and tried to wash my poor child, but the alkali water only irritated his delicate skin and his head, where it had lain on my arm, was inflamed by the constant rubbing. It began to break out in ugly blisters. I was in despair. The disappointment of not getting across the river, combined with fear that Indians were still in the neighborhood, added to my nervousness and I was exhausted nearly to the point of collapse.

The next morning after I dressed, I looked in my

small hand-mirror and it seemed my hair had turned a
grayish color. It was mostly alkali dust, but the warm
chestnut tinge never came back into it, after that day
and night of terror. My eyes looked back at me large
and hollow from the looking glass.

They decided to cross the river in spite of the
quicksand. The guide managed to pick his way
across and back on horseback, after a great deal of
floundering. They hitched up ten mules to one of the
heavily loaded baggage wagons, the teamster cracked
the whip, and in they went. But the quicksand
frightened the lead mules, who put their heads down.
The leaders disappeared entirely, then the next two and
finally the whole ten of them, irrevocably I thought.

But the officers shouted, "Cut away those mules!
Jump in there!" And the men plunged in, feeling
around under the water to cut the poor animals loose.
The mules began to crawl out on the other bank.

There lay the heavy army wagon, deep mired in the
middle of the stream, and our army chests, floating
away down the river.

"Oh! save our chests!" I cried.

"They're all right, we'll get them presently," said
Jack. In the meantime the men had unloaded the
wagon and floated the boxes and trunks to the shore,
then dismantled the wagon, which was half submerged.
They set to work to make a boat by drawing a large
canvas under the body of the wagon and fastening
it securely. This lieutenant of mine had been a
sailor-man and knew well how to meet emergencies.

On the next leg of the trip, on Stoneman's Lake Road,
we were jolted mercilessly and thrown against the sides
of the ambulance and got some bad bruises. We finally

bethought ourselves of the papoose basket, which the women at Camp Apache had given to me after Harry was born. The cradle was made of the lightest wood, covered with the finest skin of fawn, tanned with birch bark by their own hands, and embroidered in blue beads. It was their best work. They would gather each morning at nine at the half-window of our quarters to catch a glimpse of the fair baby's bath, which they thought a wonderful performance.

We placed the tired baby in the cradle, laced the sides snugly over him, and he immediately fell asleep. Jack and I sat by the campfire and mused over the hard times we were having when suddenly I heard a terrified cry from my little son. We rushed into the tent, lighted a candle, and horrors! his head and face were covered with large black ants, he was wailing helplessly and beating the air with his tiny arms.

"My God," cried Jack, "we're camped over an anthill."

I seized the child, brushed off the ants as I fled, and brought him out to the fire, where by its light I succeeded in getting rid of them all. Can you imagine how I felt when I saw those hideous, three-bodied, long-legged black ants crawling over my baby's face? Even now as I write, I cannot recall that moment without a shudder.

Towards sunset the next day, the first of May, our cavalcade reached Stoneman's Lake. We thought we had reached the limits of endurance. Then we emerged from a mountain pass and drew rein upon the high green mesa. From there we could see the lake, a beautiful blue sheet of water lying below us. It was good to our tired eyes, which had gazed upon nothing

but burnt rocks and alkali plains for so many days.
Our camp was beautiful beyond description and lay
near the edge of the mesa, where we could look down
upon the lovely lake. It was a complete surprise to us.
Ponds and lakes were unheard of in Arizona, did not
seem to exist in that drear land of arid wastes. But here
was a real Italian lake, a lake as blue as the skies above
us. We feasted our eyes and our very souls upon it. It
reminded me of when we were in Europe and visited
Lake Como, Mama and Papa.

Bailey and the guide shot some wild turkeys and we
had a supper that tasted better to us hungry travelers
than a feast at Delmonico's.

We walked to the edge of the mesa and, in the
gathering shadows of twilight, looked down into the
depths of that beautiful lake, knowing that probably
we should never see it again. This wild and grand
scenery seemed so untrod, so fresh. I remember
thinking, as we looked at the azure water, that never
had I seen anything to compare with this—but oh!
would any sane human being voluntarily go through
what I had endured on this journey, in order to look on
this wonderful scene? Indeed, in all the years I have
spent in Arizona I have never heard of the lake again.
I wonder now, did it really exist or was it an illusion,
a dream, or the mirage which appears to the desert
traveler, to satisfy him and lure him on, to quiet
his imagination, and to save his senses from utter
extinction?

When we arrived at Camp Verde, the tall Alsatian
cavalryman, who had carried the papoose cradle in his
big hands for miles, handed the baby to Mrs. O'Connell,
who was our hostess.

"Gracious goodness! What is this?" cried the bewildered woman. "Surely it cannot be your baby. You haven't turned entirely Indian, have you, amongst those wild Apaches?"

I was sorry I hadn't taken Harry out of the basket before we arrived. I didn't realize the impression it would make at Camp Verde. After all, they did not know anything about our life at Camp Apache, or our rough travels to get back from there. Here were lace-curtained windows, well-dressed women, smart uniforms, and, in fact, civilization, compared with what we had left.

We had not much rest, but proceeded to Fort Whipple, a long day's march, arriving late the next evening. The wife of the quartermaster, a total stranger to me, received us, and before we had time to exchange the usual social platitudes, took one look at the baby, and put an end to any conversation.

"You have a sick child. Give him to me." I told her some of the things that had happened and she said, "I wonder he is alive." Then she took him under her charge and declared we should not leave her house until he was well again. She understood all about nursing and day by day, under her good care, and the doctor's treatment, I saw my baby brought back to life again. Can I ever forget Mrs. Aldrich's blessed kindness?

And I think that is why I came back, Mama and Papa. There are no better people than army people, those like Mrs. Aldrich. I have learned the indomitable pluck of the enlisted men. They had taken care of my wants on long marches and performed uncomplainingly for me services usually rendered by women—cooking and laundry and taking care of our belongings. I know

*the names of all the men in Jack's "K" company and
not one but was ready to do a service for the lieutenant's wife. "K" had long been a bachelor company
and when I joined it I was a person to be pampered and
cared for. The tall Alsatian did not think it beneath
his dignity to carry Harry in his cradle across the
mountains.*

*There is my feeling for Jack, about which I cannot
write. It is too personal and too intimate, even for you,
my dear parents. Let me end with this note: To the
army with its glitter and its misery, to the post with
its discomforts, to the soldiers, to the drills, to the
bugle-calls, to the monotony, to the heat of southern
Arizona, to the uniform and the stalwart captains and
gay lieutenants who wear it, I feel the call and so I
must go. I am back again in the army. I have cast my
lot with a soldier and where he is, is home to me.*
Your loving daughter,
Mattie
    Camp McDowell
    Arizona Territory
    Christmas, 1876

So Mattie stayed in Arizona and followed Jack wherever the
army sent him. She remembered the time she lived out west with
affection and humor. She was glad she had seen a world that "vanished," but I think all worlds vanish even as we savor them.

I had loved an infant, as Mattie had. Had loved a man and been
punished for it, like Lizzie Simpson. I had been jealous, like
Armstrong. I hoped that was the only thing I had in common
with that man. I lost a baby like Susan Magoffin. I was sitting
here at Fort Whipple, as Mattie had. Remembering her brave
statement, I felt heartened myself and as light as the cottonwood

fluff that drifted from the trees at the edge of the lawn. I was hungry again. I felt the cooling air, really *felt* it on my arms. I was tired and craved a clean pillowcase under my cheek. I could savor the twilight, the old fort, and the prospect of rest.

I was alive and the lead jacket was gone. When had it lifted? In Santa Fe? At Chimayó? At the hospital? When I told Tom my story? Somewhere between Grants and Sedona?

I was alive in every pore and perfectly happy. This was what I sought.

I could keep driving. I could drive to Alaska, to Mexico City, to Nova Scotia. I could camp beside the Grand Canyon, beside Old Faithful, on Chesapeake Bay. I could pitch my tent beside the Pacific Ocean or Puget Sound or the Gulf of Mexico or the Outer Banks.

Or I could go back to Kansas City. I had the courage to go back and face my life. I could look up Tom (and apologize). Find a job. I had survived all the difficulties of the last two years, as though life had taken a stick to me. I tended to cringe a little, and cry easily, but I was standing, feet planted in reality.

I hadn't gone into some romance fantasy with Tom. I hadn't fallen apart when Dale died. I'd gotten brave enough to tell my own story.

I wondered if finding Tom would be a copout, then decided rejecting him was the copout. He had tried to be decent and I couldn't accept that. I was too used to being pushed away.

I imagined the lead jacket, sent to the cleaners, the finish buffed and all the dents hammered out. Put it away in the back of the closet.

It was high summer in the most beautiful scenery in the world. A sun as red as watermelon blazed into the mountains, pulling plum clouds after it.

Tomorrow, I'd turn around, go home, and start over again.

Acknowledgments

*T*hanks to Charlie Hammer and John Mort, better writers than I whose advice I often followed.

Thanks to libraries in New Mexico and Kansas City and all the librarians whose patience I tried.

Thanks to museums at Fort Riley, Fort Larned, Dodge City, Bent's Fort, Fort Union, and Santa Fe.

Thanks to the historians who steered me into research about army wives.

Thanks to Max Evans for his faith and Luther Wilson for his willingness to take a chance.